A
BLACK SILK CLUB
PREQUEL

VELVET
rose

G. ELENA

Edited by Cassidy Hudspeth

Spanish Proofread by Amy McLaurin-Rodriguez

English Proofread by Jenni Brady

Cover Design by Covers by Jules coversbyjules.crd.co

For a complete list of content warnings, please check out the author's website:

www.graceelenaauthor.com

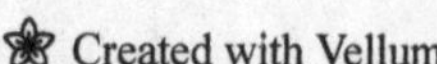 Created with Vellum

To my readers who love my forbidden, older men smut.
Be a good girl and welcome to your darkest desires.

Author's Note

Velvet Rose is a novella prequel to the Black Silk Club series. This new series is a spin-off to the standalone *In Desperate Ruin* which MUST be read first in order to understand Rosalía's backstory.

This book contains an age gap by 16 years. Rosalía and the MMC never met when she was a minor. There is absolutely no grooming in her relationship with the MMC.

If you're not personally comfortable with an age gap this big, please do not continue. Please put your mental health and your boundaries first.

Love,

Grace Elena

Content Warnings

Velvet Rose has content for a mature
audience over the age of 18.
Warnings include: bdsm club, positive kink
rep, positive sex rep, explicit sexual scenes,
slow burn, discussion of evolving eating
disorder with fmc, age gap by 16 years,
drinking, and cursing.

Playlist

Welcome to New York (Taylor's Version) by Taylor Swift

bad ones by Tate McRae

slower by Tate McRae

Bitter (feat. Trevor Daniel) by FLETCHER

God is a woman by Ariana Grande

Don't Blame Me by Taylor Swift

Read your Mind by Sabrina Carpenter

Glitch by Taylor Swift

Friends by Chase Atlantic

Paradise by Coldplay

think later by Tate McRae

Met Him Last Night (feat. Ariana Grande) by Demi Lovato

Sacrifice (feat. Jessie Reyez) by Black Atlass

Style (Taylor's Version) by Taylor Swift

Streets by Doja Cat

Deep Satin by Zach Bryan

safety net (feat. Ty Dolla $ign) by Ariana Grande

COMPLETE MESS by 5 Seconds of Summer

Welcome to

Black Silk Club

WHERE DARKNESS MEETS DESIRE

MONTHLY FEE: $5,000

NEW MEMBER VETO
FEE: $1,000

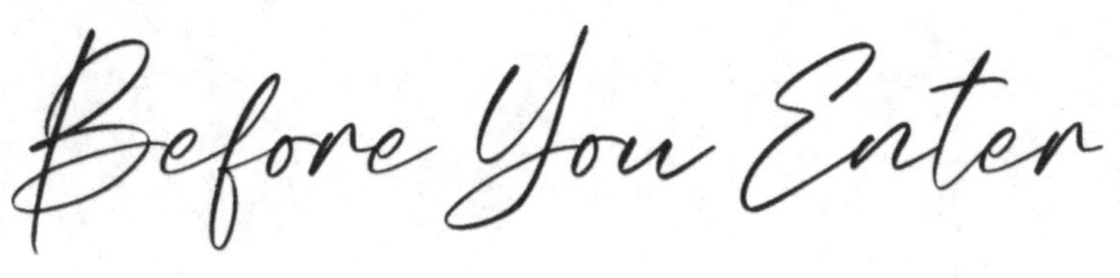

Before You Enter

CHOICE OF
VINE BRACELET
REFLECTS YOUR
PARTICIPATION FOR THE
NIGHT

CHOICE OF
FLOWER CHARM
REFLECTS YOUR KINK
ROOM FOR THE NIGHT

Vine Bracelet

SILVER:
JUST LOOKING

ROSE GOLD:
OPEN TO PARTICIPATION

GOLD:
PARTICIPATING

BLACK:
IN AN ESTABLISHED D/S RELATIONSHIP

BLUEBELL: Blindfold

CHERRY BLOSSOM: Claustrophilia

DAISY: Dominance/Submissive Training

ECHINACEA: Erotic Asphyxiation

FOXGLOVE: Food Play

GAZANIA: Gag Play

HIBISCUS: Humiliation (Degradation)

IRIS: Impact Play

KERRIA: Katoptronophilia

MAGNOLIA: Masochism

ROSE: Ropes and Bondage

SUNFLOWER: Sensory Deprivation

VIOLET: Voyeurism

WISTERIA: Wax Play

ONE

I STARE at the screen and reread the text about ten times before chucking my phone on the bed. It's not like I don't want to respond, but it's been years since I last saw him.

I vividly remember it. Graduation. He smiled from across the quad while he was hand in hand with his girlfriend. I didn't care at all and smiled back.

But this text… It's so out of the blue that it makes me curious about what might have happened with him.

There's also another part of me, the new Rosa, that doesn't give a shit about him. I ended things for a reason and have been *thriving* with my new life here.

A knock at the door surprises me, and I see Clementine peeking her head in my room. Her blonde hair is in a messy bun, and she has a food stain on her white shirt from Dahlia's mid-afternoon snack.

"You okay? I heard a very loud grunt." Her eyes fill with worry the moment she sees my phone on the bed and my clenched fists at my side. She steps into the bedroom and walks over to me, clutching my shoulders.

I sigh. "Garrett texted me, *no te preocupes*."

"Was it that bad of a text? It's been, what? Over two years since you've seen him?"

I nod.

"Yeah, *nena*. I didn't respond, though. There's no point."

Clementine is quiet, but her eyes are full of questions that she's keeping down for the sake of my own sanity. She knows I don't like to revisit things if I don't have to. As soon as I felt an inkling of change in feelings for Garrett, I knew it was a sign. I had to go–there was better for me, not just romantically, but in life.

I don't like to stay in situations that won't uplift me in better ways. And now that I'm twenty-four years old, I'm really thankful to past Rosa for leaving that behind. *Him* behind.

There's a cute giggle in the living room, and my heart warms. I smile widely before grabbing Clementine's hand and dragging her to the noise. Dahlia is on my dad's lap while he's bouncing her up and down. Her dark curls sway with every movement, and her smile matches her mother's.

"Hi, *Dally*," I coo, coming up to her. Dad watches me with bright eyes as I reach my hands out, and he lets me pick her up. Her hands are soft, reaching for my face and touching every surface.

"*Estás bien, mija*?" Dad asks as Clementine busies herself, looking through the baby bag and bringing out a rattle before handing it to me. I shake it in front of my baby sister, and she makes little grabby hands, attempting to reach for it.

"*Sí, papá*. Nothing to worry about. Did you enjoy your trip?"

He nods as he glances at my best friend, and I peer at her before her cheeks grow rosy. She's been doing that a lot since she's been here. I know how flustered she gets around my father.

It's evident in the way she has been looking at her engagement ring every second she gets.

He proposed to her the first night here, and I helped plan it alongside Frankie. It was nice to do something for the people we love, and Frankie even came to New York a little earlier than they did to help me with the proposal setup.

Clementine couldn't stop crying once he popped down on one knee. Dally giggled in my arms, and Frankie stood right behind me with his hands on my shoulders. He even leaned down and whispered in my ear that this might be one of the best moments in *his* life.

"We should tell them," Clementine breaks my thoughts, and I glance at the engaged pair, wondering what other surprises could be better than an engagement. I hear Frankie shuffling in my kitchen. Dally grabs a fist of my hair and pulls lightly, making me wince as I untangle her chubby fingers.

"Tell us what?" I ask as Dad still stays silent, but a growing smile fills his face as Clementine's eyes go from me to Dally and then to the kitchen.

"Frankie! Clementine's looking in your direction, so you need to get out here. *Ahora!*" I yell over my shoulder.

"*Ya voy,*" he shouts back before I whip my head in his direction to see his large figure entering the living room and crossing over to where we are. His brunette hair is a little longer, and the scruff he had a few days ago has grown into a mild beard. Heat flashes low in my belly with an unfamiliar urge to touch it.

I quickly dismiss it as he approaches me, looking down and smiling brightly before ruffling Dally's hair. She squirms in my arms before squealing. There's no verbal discussion from the one-year old required as I shift and move her to his arms, allowing me to cross mine over my chest and look back at my dad and best friend.

"So?" I ask.

Dad leans toward Clementine before grabbing her hand and

pulling her into his lap. She laughs before settling on him, and that's when it happens in slow motion. His hands go over her belly and rub it in slow, circular motions. I haven't even registered the collage of pictures Clementine holds in her hands until now.

"*En serio?*" I blurt, my eyes scanning my dad's hands before glancing up at them and then turning to look at Frankie, who looks just as shocked. "You didn't know?"

He shakes his head. "No idea, but I'm not surprised. *Ella no bebió nada de alcohol esta semana.*"

He's not wrong. Clementine kept drinking water while we went out to eat. Even when we got sushi, she had veggie rolls. The signs were right there, yet I didn't see them.

I jump in my place before running to Clementine and my dad, wrapping my arms around them in as big of a bear hug as my arms allow.

"*Ah, mija,*" Dad mumbles while Clementine whispers, "I hope you're not mad."

I lean back before looking at them both. "Mad? How could I be mad? Dahlia is the best thing that's happened to me, and now I get to have *two* siblings? This is the best fucking day of my life!"

Frankie gets closer as I pull myself from them, and Clementine reaches out for Dahlia. Once she's in her arms, Frankie's hand lays on my shoulder for a moment, and it feels like a sizzling hot iron making its mark. I don't even think he realizes how much this one touch affects me.

I distract myself by grabbing the picture collage my dad picked from Clementine's hands and studying the sonograms. The baby looks tucked up into Clementine's womb, and my eyes get a little teary.

"Do you know what it'll be yet?" I ask through a sniffle. Frankie's hand rubs smooth motions over my skin, and it calms me in a way. I look back at him, but with the close proximity, I have to crane my neck a little.

His brown eyes are locked on mine before his lips curl into a small smile. I lift the collage up for him to see a little more, and he leans into it. His cologne wafts my way, and it makes my head a little dizzy.

"Not yet. We want this one to be a surprise," Clementine starts. "I was thinking that the next time you come home, you can be the one to open the results, and then we can have a gender reveal party."

I nod ferociously. "Of course, *nena*. I'd be honored."

My eyes get teary again, and Frankie's hand falls from my shoulders as I close the distance between Clementine and me, wrapping her in another hug with Dahlia in the middle.

"It'll obviously be a while, but we wanted to let you both know before we went home," my dad announces.

I smile, letting the tears fall. His eyes shine from the excitement of it all, and it feels like this moment trumps the damn engagement. I worked day and night planning it with my dad and Frankie for weeks, but I know *this* will take even more planning. I want Clementine to have the best gender reveal.

"Congrats, *cabrón*," Frankie finally says, and my dad takes this moment to stand up to hug Frankie.

I give Dally a kiss on her head before kissing Clementine's forehead. Her cheeks are still rosy, and this must be that pregnancy glow they always talk about. I didn't see much of it when she was pregnant with Dahlia, but they only initially visited for a little while.

This time, I can evidently see the way her cheeks are redder, her skin is more dewy, and her figure is showing more. I guess I just preemptively thought it was because she was still occasionally breastfeeding. My knowledge with babies is low, but I've been trying to educate myself for Clementine.

I take Dahlia again from Clem before watching Frankie step

back. He glances at me for a moment before giving me a small smile and heading back to the kitchen, but not before he throws a wave and another *congrats*.

I bounce Dahlia in my arms before looking at my dad and best friend. "You guys have to drive back soon, right?"

They both nod before Clementine goes to sit on his lap, and it's the sweetest sight ever. Well, besides my baby sister.

"Yeah, Dally might like visiting you, but the road trip isn't the best. She's very fussy if you can believe it," Clementine mentions.

They're quiet for a moment as I nod. I'm going to miss them, but I'll see them soon enough. There was a moment after visiting NYC for the first time when Clementine begged me to move back. It was during the hardest part of her pregnancy when she just really needed her soul sister, so I hopped on a plane and stayed for two weeks before going back home. I ended up having to come back to Sunny Cove a month later for her labor. That's when Dad asked me the same question —if I could move back.

I knew they didn't mean any harm by it, but I had to tell them that Sunny Cove wasn't my home anymore. It was theirs, and that was okay. I love New York City, and I've grown so much in the past two years of living here. More than I ever could have if I stayed in that small town.

Clementine watches me for a moment before giving me a reassuring smile, and even Dahlia rests her fingers on my cheek as if they both can read my mind.

"You okay with Frankie hanging around here for a little?" Dad asks with a raised brow and humor in his voice. I look at him and roll my eyes.

That's when I hear dishes clanging, and I know Frankie's already making himself at home again. He's been doing that anytime we come back to my apartment as a group. It brings me back to the other night before Clementine and Dad arrived. The moment I got the notification from my doorman that he was here in the lobby. I ran down (well, used the elevator), and he literally pulled me in for a hug, picked me up, and twirled me around until I was screaming.

It was different from the other times I saw him. There was something about this that made me keep overthinking things. But I've been dismissing every thought in hopes that he can't read my mind.

He's my Uncle Frankie!

Even though he's not my dad's brother by blood, I still see him that way. I *have* to, at least. He's like family, even if lines have become blurry recently on my end. But I have to remind myself that his lines are very much opaque with a damn neon sign above saying "will never cross."

I'm working a late shift tonight and just wanted to get my clothes ready until I saw that text from Garrett. My head snaps to the kitchen, where Frankie is on his phone. His legs are spread out comfortably on the chair. He's got his brows scrunched, and his lower lip tugs between his teeth.

I nod at Dad. "I think I'll be okay. He promised me dinner tonight before I head into work, so I can't say no to that."

"Your roommate isn't coming home soon?" Clementine asks, and I shake my head. Luisa's working a double at the same club I work at, so she's been gone since one this afternoon.

"Nope, we've got the place to ourselves. I hope you guys enjoyed it better than the last apartment."

"I like this one way better, *mija*," Dad answers. My last apartment was a nightmare where the maintenance was shitty, the landlord didn't care about safety, and my roommate was a slob.

I'm just grateful I found better this year to continue living in New York. The moment my coworker, Luisa, told me she was looking for a roommate, I immediately jumped at the offer.

"I want to visit again, maybe alone?" Clementine speaks up.

She looks at Dad, who smiles brightly. "You'd enjoy a whole week alone with Dahlia, wouldn't you?"

He nods. "A whole week *con mi flor? Por supuesto.* In fact, we should start planning that so I can get all her favorite foods."

"Like what?" I ask with a laugh as Dahlia touches my face again, and I pat her bottom before shifting my feet and bouncing her slowly.

"Those damn puffs! He gets her all the flavors, and I have to remind him that those are *snacks,* not full meals." Clementine huffs.

"She's like her mother," Dad argues with a laugh. "I can't say no to her. Especially with those pretty eyes and chubby cheeks."

I look at Dahlia, whose eyes match her mother's. She looks up at me in wonder, and my heart melts. "If she asked me to steal the Declaration of Independence, I would right this second," I agree.

Dad and Clementine laugh as we hear a faint grunt from Frankie in the kitchen. I take that as my cue to see if he's okay and lean down to give Dahlia back to her parents. Once I'm nearing the kitchen, Frankie looks up from his phone and shifts a little in his seat to straighten his posture.

"Everything okay?"

He nods and runs a hand over his growing beard. His brown eyes glance at me briefly before moving to the kitchen table. "Yeah, just can't seem to find a place for dinner. *Lo siento,* Rosita. Most of them have reservations that are completely booked."

I give him a smile before closing the distance and giving him a side hug to the best of my ability while he's sitting down. I squeeze his shoulder. "It's okay. I think I know a place that might let us steal a table."

Frankie huffs and his whole body moves underneath me. His broad shoulders are strong, and I stand back up, keeping one hand on him. He turns to look at me for a moment, but he's still got that grumpy face on.

"What?" I ask, narrowing my eyes.

He shakes his head. "*Nada.* You just look a lot like your dad right now."

I give my best fake gag and even gesture, pointing my finger down my throat. "Ugh, don't bring up my dad."

"What, why?" He halfheartedly laughs, but it echoes in this small kitchen and seems to even vibrate inside my body with how close I am.

"Nothing," I start, but Frankie leans in a little closer as if he wants in on the secret. I sigh and continue. "He's just been asking a lot about my job, and it's a *bar* job. Not really something a father wants to know details about…"

"Slinging cocktails and letting older men hit on you?" He winks, and I playfully slap his shoulder.

"No! Well, you know…" I pause, and he smiles brazenly. I roll my eyes. "How else will I get paid the way I do to afford this apartment? But don't you dare tell him that."

His smile fades for a moment as he's deep in thought. "Just let me know if any of those old fuckers get too close. I'll be in New York for a little. I might not be your father, but I'll protect what's–"

I smirk. "What's *yours*?" He's silent for a moment before I add, "That's such a dad line. Yuck."

Don't cross a line. Don't cross the very blurry line, Rosalía…

He scoffs and smiles again. "Rosita, don't make me feel old like those creeps at your so-called job." He pauses. "But, yes. If that's what it'll take to get them to back off. Then, you're damn right about that. I'll protect what's mine."

His words ping-pong inside my head, echoing loudly. It feels like there's a sudden shift in the air. I can't tell if it's just *me* with this unfamiliar feeling. An electric current flows through us where my hand is still placed on his shoulder. I want to move it, but I don't. It feels harder to breathe, and we just keep staring at each other for the next few seconds before we hear Dahlia giggle in the other room.

I jump and remove my hand from his shoulder. He clears his throat before scraping his chair back and standing up. He's inches taller than me, similar in height to my six-foot-four father. I crane my neck just a tad to look at him before he walks past me. But I catch the way he glides his hand over the top of my back and squeezes my shoulder. My whole body seems to shudder at the contact.

Huh.

TWO

THE RESTAURANT IS DIMLY LIT, and I forget that it's Frankie's first time here, and he can barely read the menu. He's squinting his eyes, looking grumpier by the second.

I let out a giggle and he cranes his neck to look down at me, making me zip my lips.

"What?"

"Need a flashlight?" I ask, giving him a shit-eating grin.

He rolls his eyes before leaning closer to me, his knee bumping into mine. Although I didn't mind that we had to sit at the bar, it meant we'd have to sit side by side. It isn't much of a bother, except we're all the way at the end, where I've got my left shoulder pressed against the wall, and his big frame almost engulfs mine in the process.

He bumps shoulders with me, and the length of his thigh presses against mine. The weather isn't too cold, so I've got on my signature black skirt and sheer tights. The skirt rides up a little, so I jolt when his pants make contact. He's got on black dress pants and a dark maroon dress shirt with the sleeves pulled up to show off the muscles in his forearms.

Not that I'm looking.

I'm not sure what the hell is going on, but there's something and it's making it harder to be around Frankie than I'd like to admit.

Tension.

Something I've tried so desperately to push down, especially when it came to the man next to me.

And it didn't miraculously start today. My move to New York didn't help one bit. Something I never thought would happen to me regarding my dad's *best friend*. It caught me by surprise the first time, and I could remember it like it was yesterday.

His knee bumps into mine again and knocks me out of the past, and I look up at him and give him a smirk. "Here," I say before pulling out my phone and turning up the brightness on the screen before flipping it over to bring light to the menu in his hands. It's better than shining a damn flashlight and causing a scene or getting judgy looks from the bartenders.

I know the bartender tonight, Hannah, wouldn't mind, but she'd definitely laugh at Frankie. I would, too, but right now, my nerves are high-strung for some reason.

He leans into the menu under the bright light, and his stubbled chin accidentally touches my knuckle, making me pull away instinctively. His free hand grabs my wrist and pulls me back to the menu.

"Like that," he breathes. "Perfect."

I gulp, unsure of what the hell I should do. With my hand outstretched over his menu, I sit there, and his fingers wrap around my wrist perfectly. Images of unthinkable things come to mind.

I blame my job. Lately, it's got me thinking a lot more about my *preferences* in the bedroom. Like a man with his calloused, big hands grabbing my wrists, pulling them above me, and tying them on the headboard. It's not my fault that Frankie's hand fit the image perfectly—

"I'll get the caviar," he finally says.

I raise a brow. "Going all out, huh?"

He laughs, and it vibrates in the air and through his hold on me. "I'm in New York City, baby!"

The nickname fell so easily off his lips, and I swallowed a thick wad of cotton that developed in my mouth. He doesn't seem to notice, and I pull my phone back, turning it off before chucking it in my purse. I shift a little in my barstool.

"I'll get the roast chicken, and we can share," I tell him.

"Fine by me, Rosita." He finally turns to me and smiles. It seems to ease the thick tension because I smile back at him.

We flag down Hannah before ordering another round of drinks as well as what we've decided on for dinner. Conversation flows well like it always does with Frankie, mostly about my life here in New York and Dahlia. We love her so much, and he catches me up on everything.

Our food comes soon after that, and we take turns trying the caviar before diving into the roast chicken. The flavors are so well done that I can't help but let out a soft moan while biting into the next piece of chicken. I widen my eyes before looking at him, and he chuckles and shakes his head.

"What?" I laugh, nudging him with my elbow. I hit his side, and he makes a small *oof* noise before settling back in his seat. He looks at me before picking up a piece, popping it in his mouth, and swallowing before answering.

"It makes me happy seeing you happy here. *En esta ciudad*."

The conversation seems to have tilted to something that brings that same tension from before. I swallow any remnant pieces of chicken I'm chewing on before deciding on my next words very carefully.

Blurry lines. Don't. Cross.

"Thanks, Frankie. I know my dad was super worried about me moving. But I love it here and had a good feeling about it even before I decided on it."

"And I can tell. I've always wanted you to follow your heart, and now look at you, Rosalía."

I swallow, looking at him. He's never called me that. Only Rosita. The air has shifted once again, and I lean into it—into him.

It might be the two glasses of wine in my system mixed with an empty stomach aside from this roast chicken, but I don't care. My inhibition screams for contact.

His eyes cast down to my lips before lifting back to my eyes. He leans into it a little, and I'm practically falling off my stool as I nudge myself closer, pressing my knees into his outer thigh.

"Look at *you*," he whispers, almost to himself. The heat seems to increase in my body, and I know if there were lights in this restaurant, he'd see me looking like a tomato. The angel on my shoulder is screaming at me to stop, scoot back into my stool, and continue my meal.

But the devil on my shoulder tells me to place my hand on his thigh. And so I do.

He watches me intently before licking his lips and leaning more into our personal bubble.

"Rosalía, what are you doing?" he mutters under his breath.

"I-I don't know, but—"

Before I can reply, Hannah comes up to us and asks if we want another round. My hand on his thigh squeezes from the surprise, and a groan slips from his lips. I bite my lip to keep myself from giggling before looking at Hannah and shaking my head.

"Actually, I think we're ready for the check," he says a little too loudly. Hannah looks at me before nodding and heading to the register to close our tab. I scoot back into my stool, pulling my hand away from his thigh in the process, and I swear I hear a grumble of disappointment.

I glance up at Frankie, and he still has a smile on his face as he reaches for his drink and finishes it. Hannah quickly brings the check, and Frankie pulls out his wallet as I'm about to grab my card from my purse.

"It's fine, Rosita, I've got it."

It feels like my whole body deflates, alongside my ego, with the way he goes back to calling me Rosita.

I need him to call me Rosalía one more time. But he's already cracked the illusion of what was going on just between us. The bubble has popped, and it's like I can finally hear what's around me. The noise is loud, and I want to leave. The sensory overload is making my skin crawl.

"Thanks," I mutter a little too harshly before Hannah comes and takes the bill. She glances at me, and I give her a tight smile. She quickly returns with his card, and I peek as he signs and leaves a hefty tip.

Woah. I knew my dad made good money with his contracting company, but I didn't think it was *that* much. Unless in the last year Frankie quit and got a different job that I wasn't informed about it. Or won the lottery.

"Ready?" he asks, turning to me. I nod quickly before hopping off the stool and almost colliding into him as he does the same. His movement is much more graceful than mine, but he has to grab my shoulders to keep me from falling.

"Sorry," I mumble before he gives me a warm smile that spreads like wildfire in my veins.

He gestures for me to go first, so I lead the way out of the restaurant until we're on the street. A few cars zip by, and I turn to see him stuffing his hands in the pockets of his dress pants.

"My shift starts soon," I say. I'd love for him to walk me to work, but I don't need him telling my dad where I work. I don't need *Frankie* to know where I work. I've kept this secret for so long, but it's for the best.

It would be way more than I could handle if they ever found out. I love my job, but it's not ideal and is often frowned upon once others find out.

"Want me to walk you? My friend is in town, and I don't have to meet him for another hour," Frankie starts. I shake my head, and there's a clear disappointment in his face that makes me want to reverse time.

"It's not too far." I think of a quick lie. "My coworker lives just down the street, so I can walk with her. We're working the same shift."

It's a white lie. Willow does work tonight, but she's already there.

He nods before taking a deep breath and stepping closer. I hold my breath for a moment, looking up at him. I see his dark eyes study me. He's so damn beautiful. I just never took the time to see it.

Or maybe I was stuck in the thought of seeing him as close family. But the time I've spent in New York has changed things and how I see things. How I care about things.

Maybe that's why I'm still okay about my best friend and dad. It's just something I'm cool with, and there was a reason. This job is perfect for me, and it all makes sense.

Forbidden aspects and secrets have become my favorite things. My coworker Willow loves to talk about Clementine and my dad whenever she gets the chance ever since I told her about them. My roommate, Luisa, even agreed and always wants to stay updated on all things Clementine and Dad.

They'd crack up if I told them about my current predicament. I haven't told a soul about the slow glances, the soft touches, and the forbidden feeling I've had more times than I can count with Frankie. I know it's probably all one-sided, but I'm falling deep into it.

Maybe it's a genetic thing, now that I think about it. My dad went for my best friend. And now I'm fiending for his best friend.

"What are you thinking about?" He breaks my thoughts with

his question, and I remember that I'm face to face with him. I chew on the inside of my cheek before smiling.

"*Nada*. Just stupid things. I've got to go, though. You'll be okay?"

He laughs. "Usually, it's *me* asking that. Yeah, I'll be fine, Rosita. Let me know if you need anything. I'm a call away. Like I told you, I'll be in New York for a little."

I nod before he takes a step back, and I do the same. It's like an invisible rope has been tied around us and loosens with each step, yet still tethered. I don't want to leave for some reason, but I have to go to work.

I've got a long night ahead of me, and it's not helping seeing Frankie like this. He raises a brow as if he wants to say something but doesn't. He turns on his heels and starts walking in the opposite direction. He steals a glance when he's almost halfway down the block, and my cheeks burn when I realize I haven't moved an inch.

"*Calmáte, Rosalía*," I tell myself before I turn and head towards work. It's a twenty-minute walk, but it allows me to clear my head.

THREE

BY THE TIME I make it to the front of the bar, I see Ronan. He gives me a nod as I approach, and he's scanning me already for any potential weapons. I roll my eyes.

"I don't have anything, you know that."

He smiles, his perfect teeth almost blinding me. His neck and chest tattoos are peeking through his open-collared shirt. His work attire is a little different than the other security guys. They usually wear a black shirt with *SECURITY* labeled on the back. But he's wearing a rich purple dress shirt that looks like it's made of silk. How fitting.

I look up at him again, and he laughs. "I know, *princesa*. Just doing my job so the big boss can see."

"Aren't you the boss?" I ask. He's the head of security here, and it's his security company.

He shakes his head and throws his thumb toward the purple neon glowing sign above us.

Blackbird Silhouettes

"River?" I ask, noting *my* boss's name—the bar and secret club owner.

He nods before crossing his arms over his chest. With this movement, I see his shirt ride up a little to showcase his holster on the waistband of his dress pants. I've never seen Ronan have to utilize his gun, but then again, I moved down to the club just three months into working here.

I used to be a waitress on the main bar floor until my roommate put in a good word for me to River, and now I'm living my dreams, financially at least.

"I'll let you know if any of your regulars show," he states. I give him a smile before slipping through the black door and into the bar.

There aren't many patrons in the bar, just a few stragglers at the counter, and then a few couples are drinking—most likely finishing up their dinner dates. The floor pulses a little underneath my feet, meaning the shows have started downstairs.

Willow said she wanted to start doing shows the other day, so I wonder if she'll be up on the stage tonight. I also can't remember if we have an event. I have felt so scatterbrained since Dad, Clementine, and Frankie visited.

I head toward the back, waving to our bartenders before meeting the other security guy, Terry, near the back of the bar. He's manning the door and gives me a once over before nodding and letting me through. It's pitch black until I head down the lengthy stairs and turn the corner, seeing the purple glow of *another* neon sign.

Black Silk Club

The music seems to intensify as I enter the sex club, and I see girls already dancing on stage with masks and members, wealthier than the people upstairs, watching from a distance in their velvet chairs. Their bracelets reflect brightly under the lights.

I quickly ruffle through my purse for a simple black eye mask and put it over my face before heading through the club hallway until I'm near the employee's lounge. I keep my fancier masks in my locker. I never take those outside of the club.

The music continues to pulse as I enter the employee's lounge and see some girls getting ready in front of their vanities. Angelique is curling her hair to the far right at our hair station, and Veronica is fixing her dress. Willow is finishing up picking a garter up from our center table before giving me a wave and walking out.

I take my time saying hello to the girls before I find the lockers down a small hall to the left of the lounge, quickly stuff my purse, and grab my main mask. It's a delicate black lace detailed mask with purple silk ties. There's a mirror in my locker that I use to put it on before I freshen up a little with the products I have stashed.

My shift is usually four hours, but if a girl is out sick or more girls get called into rooms, I stay longer for the other members. Most days, I typically work the front of the house since I came from upstairs and have cocktail experience. I like conversing with our members when giving them their drinks and encouraging them to come back with a bracelet. I also like to tell them who the best girls are to get rooms with based on their bracelet color and flower charms.

River has been wanting me to get more comfortable and see if there were any rooms I'd like to try either on my own or with a trusted member, but I've yet to really experience it. I've tried *exploring* more in my bedroom than here, but an inkling of curiosity makes me want to push past that comfort zone, grab a member, and bring them to one of the many rooms we have down here.

But first I want to trust the members and make sure I feel

comfortable enough to be in a room alone with them. I went on a few dates with a member *outside* the club–that didn't last long and we only hooked up a few times. The idea of going into a room with him freaked me out and I wasn't ready, but he didn't push.

My coworkers make it seem so easy to find a regular. They've built amazing relationships with our clientele, and I hope to be there someday, but I'm still super hesitant.

"Rosalíaaaaa, are you here?" River's voice drifts through the lounge before it gets louder, and I see a peek of her jet-black hair leaning over a wall to my right. Even though we try to keep to our club nicknames when working, we converse in the back with our real ones. Like now.

"Yeah, boss?" I ask, spinning around to see her finally show herself. Her main attire is a purple silk dress with a black mask and clear heels. She's inadvertently matching Ronan.

River's got members of her own, but I've never seen her go back with any of them since working here. She's our main Dominatrix.

She must do it all when the club is closed and on her own hours.

Her dark red lips press together before she looks me up and down, but it's not in a condescending way. Her lips curl into a smile.

"I want you to be more involved tonight. Maybe the stage?"

My eyes bug out of their sockets, and my heart picks up its pace for a moment. "What? The stage?"

She nods. "If you're up for it, of course. I see the way you look at the girls up there. You look at them in *envy* and—"

"You saw that?" I can feel the heat rise to my cheeks, but I don't lift my hands to rub them. River smiles even more broadly before nodding.

"And curiosity, Rosalía. It's okay to do it at your own pace. It's okay to go steady. But I don't want my girls here feeling less than confident in their bodies. It deserves to be worshipped."

I smile sheepishly. I don't have a body like a Victoria's Secret model by any means, but I attempt to appreciate her words. River loves to embrace the human body. She wants all her girls to be confident and take what they need to feel satiated. That ultimately means that we need to be able to be satiated *sexually*.

River made sure to vet all club members to the extent that if we were to be asked to meet outside of the club, we'd be respected in every avenue, or else their membership could be revoked, and any legal action would be taken with full support.

I've yet to hear any horror stories about members who forced a club girl to do something she didn't want to do. Or anything terrible happening *outside* of the club.

Having so many rules inside *Black Silk* helps keep things maintainable. For instance, alcohol and drugs are strictly prohibited for members who participate in rooms or are alone with the girls. Only members who want to watch and have no interest in participating in anything are allowed alcohol. We can tell who's participating or not by their vine bracelets.

Silver means no participation, just looking. Rose Gold means interest and possibly participating. Gold is for members who know they will participate. Black is for the members who are already in Dominant and Submissive relationships, so we don't really converse with them. They come to the club with their partners for privacy in our rooms.

The flower charms on the rose gold and gold bracelets indicate which kink room the members want to utilize for the night.

I briefly think back to the member I got close with outside the club. Reeve *always* respected my boundaries when we were together. Both outside and inside. He paid for everything, spoiled me when I didn't even ask for it, and the sex was—well, it was incredible. I can't deny *that*. But something was missing for me to continue in both the outside world and in Black Silk—a spark, so to speak.

"Well?" River's voice breaks me out of my thoughts, and I shift my weight onto one foot.

"I know, but I don't know if tonight is my night." Plus, the idea of dancing makes my stomach churn. I've never danced in front of a man and having this mask on doesn't make it any different. "I'm pretty tired from my dad visiting and I feel bloated, just having dinner with my dad's best—"

"Sounds like excuses," she apprehends me with a raised brow.

I want to roll my eyes at her, but I know she's right. She's not pushing me. She wants me to find the confidence to step up and do something I internally want to try.

I *want* to get on that damn stage and own the night. I *want* to have members flocking to me to have time in a room whether it's an hour or even more. The money would be a plus.

Coming to this job as a bartender was fine, but now that I'm downstairs, I second-guess everything. It's not even intentional, and no one knows, at least I hope not. It's like a mental game of whether or not I feel my best. I've found myself feeling less than compared to the amazing girls here. But I know it's just *me*. The girls are great and compliment me any chance they get, but my mind plays tricks on me and makes me think it's not true.

River hasn't mentioned anything, and the girls don't bring it up if they have noticed. Luisa hasn't brought it up either in the club or back at our apartment.

Having dinner tonight with Frankie made me forget it all. I didn't check my alcohol intake and if the sugar content was too much. I didn't give a damn about stuffing my face with a roast chicken.

And the way Frankie looked at me all day today made me forget the whole plan I conceived about working out until I burned all those calories.

So really, I don't even know what is holding me back from doing more in this club.

Probably myself.

River takes a step closer to me, and her hazel eyes bore into mine. She lifts a finger, presses it under my chin, and lifts until I'm forced to look at her.

"You never know what might happen tonight."

I stay still, watching her eyes search mine. I gulp, unsure what to say. My fingers itch, and I lose all my confidence right there. Sweat is starting to creep at the nape of my neck, and I want to freshen up all over again.

Without a moment's notice, River drops her finger and smiles. "Trust me, Rosalía." She pauses. "You know I only want what's best for you, right? You don't have to try it tonight, but I'd like you to think about it."

I nod. "I know. I trust you, River."

"Good. You deserve to be worshipped in every way. I want my line blowing up with calls to get access to this club because of a pretty little thing like *you* making my members want even a *peek* at you. You deserve that glory."

Do I?

I look at her before she takes a step back. I take a deep breath, watch her turn on her heels, and leave the room. My gaze moves to the mirror in my locker, and I watch my reflection.

The way my curled locks frame my face and the mask that covers almost my whole face. My eyes are bright against the black lace, and even my boobs are peeking out a little from the top I'm wearing.

Change.

The devil's voice of reason is starting to sound more like River's advocate, and I want to lean into it. There's a lilac lace corset that accentuates my waist as well as pushes my breasts to look even bigger than they are. Right under it is a black silk mini-skirt and clear pumps.

I contemplate staying in the clothes I'm in, but I want what River mentioned. I *deserve* the attention and members to fawn over me. The thrill of it all and the prospect of having members drool over me is what I need tonight.

My thoughts drift to Frankie for a moment, and the silliest idea of wondering how he'd react if he saw me in this ensemble fills my brain.

Would he like it?

Would he rather rip it to shreds before worshipping my body?

Without a second thought, I grab the outfit and slam the locker shut before heading to the changing room.

FOUR

ANGELIQUE HAD to tighten the corset, but her affirming comments made me feel even better about my choice to change outfits.

"You're going on stage or participating in our raffle tonight?" Kiki, another girl working tonight, asks.

I see her in the reflection of one of the floor-length mirrors as Angelique is fixing the back of my mask. She said she wanted to blend the ties with my curled hair, so I'm letting her work her magic.

"I didn't know there was a raffle tonight," I answer. Angelique nods as she finishes her work and pats the crown of my head. I turn to thank her before looking at Kiki, whose brunette hair is swaying with her movements as she fixes her dress.

"Mhm," she starts. "It happens every quarter. I thought you knew."

I knew *Black Silk* operated a raffle every quarter, but I didn't think it was tonight. That's how I met Reeve. Well, not exactly. He was here for the raffle, dragged and vetoed by another veteran member, and then we met as I was serving him drinks.

He was just looking and not participating, and that's how we struck up a conversation for the rest of the night.

I've yet to participate in any of the raffles. They're not too *out there* with what they entail. We don't fixate too much on the Dominant and Submissive roles between members and workers for the raffles. River likes focusing more on exploring your sexual desires and deepest secrets. It's supposed to be a fun time for both the members and workers.

It's definitely what sets us apart from other clubs.

We have our set rates for different rooms, and if the girl wants to request more while she's working, then she can. Even at the annual auction, the bids start off however much the girl wants, and then the members can bid for more. River is very pro-know-your-worth.

As a cocktail waitress, I can't really complain that I'm not getting my fair share of money. I've made plenty of tips from just walking around the club offering drinks and water.

"I guess I forgot that River mentioned it," I respond.

Kiki's golden sheer dress shines underneath the lights in the lounge as she rounds the corner of the center table to head out to the main floor.

"See you out there," Kiki calls. Angelique is fixing the pieces of hair that frame her face before she follows Kiki.

I'm the last one here, and I look once more at the surrounding mirrors. I take a deep breath and watch the girl in the mirror straighten her posture and puff out her chest a little. A flash of something glittery catches my attention from the center table. It's a purple garter with silver glitter. It'll match the corset perfectly.

Another thought of a possible *someone* catching it with his teeth and pulling it down my body causes an unsolicited moan to leave my lips.

No, Rosalía. Stop, stop, stop—

Before another voice of reason can stop me, I snatch the

garter off the counter and slip it over my thigh. It's tight, but the way the light catches each fleck of glitter makes me warm inside. Like a flutter of butterflies at the pit of my belly. And even lower. An ache between my legs.

I'M on the main floor, where I catch the bartender's eyes, who seems to be calling me over. We usually have two bartenders down here, but there seems to be only one tonight.

Once I reach the counter of the bar, Evan smiles at me. His bright, green eyes are illuminated with the white mask surrounding the top of his face. He's not wearing a mask covering his whole face tonight, which isn't too rare in the bartender's case. The girls are strictly told to wear masks covering most of our faces, eyes, and noses until we get to the private rooms, where we can choose to take them off.

"You've got a few orders," he states with a sing-song voice and nods his head toward the counter where drinks are waiting to be sent to members. I look behind me quickly to see the place starting to get busier by the minute.

Girls are already walking with their chosen club members to various hidden hallways that lead to private rooms. Each hallway is designated for a particular kink that glows the color of the flowers.

"Thanks, E," I say before grabbing as many of the drinks as I can. They have little umbrella toothpicks in each one with a faint number to tell me which seat it's for. Just something Evan and I started doing once I started as his drink runner. It got too confusing the busier we got throughout the night, so one day, we came up with this system.

I head to seat 24 and hand the whiskey on the rocks to the

member whose eyes are set on Angelique. I make sure to glance at his wrist for the silver vine bracelet.

Angelique's dance on stage is hypnotizing, and her hips sway to the music. The guy thanks me before giving me a once-over and then takes a sip of the drink. I give him a slight nod before heading to the next two seats who ordered water.

By the time I'm back at the bar, Evan has one more drink ready for me. It's a snakebite shot, and I visibly shudder.

"Who the hell ordered this?" I ask Evan, lifting the shot glass toward him as he shakes another order midair.

He shrugs. "No idea, but his voice was very husky, and I almost proposed right there."

I laugh. "You didn't get his name?"

"No, I want you to do that," he winks, and I almost miss it. I give him a look before spinning on my heels and almost bump into someone. The shot *almost* gets dumped on the nice suit in the process, but I stabilize myself just in time.

"Sorry, sir!" I apologize quickly and look up to meet familiar bright blue eyes. The smile he dons is memorable and there's no mistaking it's Reeve Preston. I could spot him miles away, even with his mask on.

His build is wide, his height almost six-five, and although things ended between us, there was no denying the way he still made me feel.

"Rosalía, I didn't know you were working tonight." His voice drags into more of a whispered question, and I nod. I'm glad he's whispering my real name since I tend to go by a nickname for privacy and security with new members I don't trust yet. I trust Reeve, though, wholeheartedly.

"Didn't think you'd be stopping by tonight, Reeve," I respond, sidestepping him for a moment before he catches my elbow softly. His hand is calloused, and his fingers are long enough to wrap around my arm easily.

"Me either. Surprised to see you working tonight. Are you doing the raffle this time?"

Memories of meeting him the last time we had a raffle flood my mind, and I shake my head. "Nope, still not doing it. Are you planning to participate?"

He nods. "Yep. Thought it'd be a nice change. If you were part of the raffle, I'd wish on the luckiest star I got chosen."

I give him the best smile. "That's sweet, but that won't be happening. Maybe in the future."

We stood there idly, and I could feel the slight increase of awkward tension. The snakebite in my hand seems to be getting warmer by the second, and I don't want to keep the member waiting.

I lift the glass and gesture toward the main floor. "I've gotta–"

"Right." He smiles. "It was nice seeing you again. Maybe we can–"

Before he can finish, Evan whistles at me and flicks his hand toward the floor. The drink. Right.

"Maybe," I whisper before giving Reeve one last look. He looks handsome tonight in his suit, but like I realized not so long ago… There wasn't more to it for me.

I didn't come to New York to be stuck in the same predicament that I was in with Garrett.

I wanted more, and I *deserved* more.

As I head toward seat 13, my eyes glance around the club. More girls came for their shift to help with the increased clientele tonight for the raffle. About forty girls work either in the raffle, on the floor, or in the rooms.

The member waiting on his snakebite is staring at the stage, his back to me. His shoulders are broad, and the dress shirt is dark against the bright purple lights above. His brunette hair is swept in gorgeous waves, and I watch slowly as he lifts a hand to run through it. That's when I notice the dress shirt sleeve rolled up, showcasing delicious muscles and veins.

I swallow, unsure why this is happening. *I need to get laid.*

I also notice that he's wearing a silver vine bracelet.

"Here's your snakebite, sir," I announce as I round his chair. His thighs are thick as ever, and an image of me attempting to climb him comes to the forefront of my mind.

I blame seeing Reeve. And Frankie, no doubt. Those encounters are turning my mind to mush and making me want some kind of release.

You just want to let go—tonight. The devil practically screams in my left ear.

The man turns his head and watches me slowly as I bend at the waist and bring the shot up close to him. Fuck, he's handsome. He's got a growing beard that looks like it'd do some damage in between my legs.

He leans forward, causing his knee to bump into mine. A noise escapes my lips, and he grabs the shot, engulfing my hand in the process.

Calloused, large hands that feel like heaven. He pulls the shot out of my hand, and I have to remember how to use my limbs, making him almost pull me down onto him in the process.

"Easy there, *Ángel*," he mutters under his breath. It's husky, with a hint of an accent.

Evan was right.

"I'm fine," I answer, pulling my hand to my side and straightening my posture. The lights overhead are spotlights and move away from above him to shine directly over me. I squint a little until they move back to another part of the club.

His eyes are on mine, gliding over my body. But not in an uncomfortable way. It's a slow drag of his irises from top to bottom before settling on my face again. Everything in me heats up.

All this for a man in a damn mask.

My fingers find the garter for a moment and play with it, making his eyes follow along. That's when he adjusts his position on the leather chair. I can't help but focus on his midsection, then lower. And lower. To his crotch. My eyes widen, watching for a moment before I glance back up to his face.

You know when guys wear sweatpants, and you just *know* they're big? Well, you can tell in dress pants as well. And with the way he's sitting, I can see the perfect outline of his crotch against the fabric. I can't imagine how big he'd really be if he's aroused.

Stop thinking about a member's cock size, Rosa.

I mumble nonsense under my breath before taking a step back. He pulls the shot to his lips before throwing his head back and taking it. He doesn't wince at all from the bitter whiskey.

"I can take that if you're done," I say quickly, reaching my hand out.

His eyes stay on mine as he presses the shot glass into my palm. "Thank you, *Ángel*."

My ovaries are not doing well with this man and his husky voice calling me angel. I give him a nod before making my way back to the bar as quickly as I can. I slump into a barstool and let out a heavy sigh.

Evan is talking to another girl before heading back to me. He taps the counter, and I give him a side-eye.

"I'm guessing you didn't get his name?"

I shake my head. "He called me angel."

"What?"

I nod. "In Spanish."

Evan smirks and leans over to pat my arm. "You should ask him if he's willing to get a room."

"What?!" My eyes almost bug out of their sockets. "Evan!"

"I'm just kidding, Rosemary," he calls me by my club nickname before continuing. "Take your time! The members will always be here. Well, I hope *that* one is."

"Who knows," I say with a shrug.

I glance over my shoulder to where the mystery Snakebite member is. He's not in his seat anymore, but it's not like anyone can take it for themselves. You're given a specific seat anytime you come to the club, so he's lucky number 13 for the remainder of the night.

"Earth to Rosemary," Evan calls out, snapping his fingers near my ear. I whip my head back to him, and I stick my tongue out.

"He can't tonight. He ordered liquor, remember?"

He laughs. "I'm still shocked you're not participating in the raffle tonight even if he isn't."

"I don't feel—" I try to say, but he lifts a finger to hush me. It also seems to hush the nagging thoughts of what I'm scared to admit is happening to me.

The more these thoughts grow, the less I feel like the confident and secure Rosalía that could push them away. It's all so new that I don't even know how to navigate what's going on.

"Do I need to pull you away and talk? I don't want to see any of my work friends struggling with something that can lead to something serious."

My lips twitch into a smile, but it's forced. "I'm fine, E. Really. It's nothing to worry about. I'm just bloated, that's all."

"I'm always here if you need to talk." He reminds me.

The truth is at the tip of my tongue, almost turning sour where I want to spit it out. I don't know what's gotten into me. I want to talk about it. I almost did with Clementine this weekend.

I think I have an eating disorder. Crazy, right?

But I didn't want to ruin anyone's vacation. I wanted to hint it to Frankie even, see what he thought. I felt like I could talk to him even more than my own best friend or father.

My thoughts seem to drift more toward him, and I sigh. Evan is still watching me before he pats my hand and then heads to work on more drinks.

I swivel on the barstool to watch the club. The raffle is about to start at the stroke of midnight. I glance at seat 13 once more, and he's back. As if he can feel my stare, he turns his head slowly and I hop off the barstool to head to another section.

Fuck, I need to stop staring. And the only way is to get out of his line of sight.

The voice of a girl who usually sets up the stage for events like this fills the speakers around the club, and she takes center stage to start the raffle. I sulk in a dark corner and stand to watch the night unfold.

FIVE

LUISA PLOPS down in the seat in front of me, handing over a plate of cookies. Her brunette hair is curled today with the front pieces pinned to the back with a long, white bow. She has a black sheer dress with a silk white slip underneath and black leggings.

She's the definition of cute, fashionable, and *quaint coquette girl* all wrapped in one.

"*Aquí tienes*," she says before I take it.

"You didn't have to, *gracias*," I say softly.

I had a wild hangover this morning after drinking too much with Willow and Luisa on our couch last night. It's been over a week since the raffle and the club has been so busy, so we had a much needed catch up night.

She waves her hand before pausing and taking a cookie from the plate, biting into it. "*Es deliciosa*, I know the baker who works here."

I nod before picking up a cookie. I inspect it for a second before I realize she's watching me. I nibble on it, letting the chocolate goodness fill my tastebuds. The noise around the coffee shop is minimal but enough to worsen my pounding headache.

Luisa's manicured hands start to flip through a magazine she got from the front of the cafe. She tries to keep up with the latest fashion and tabloids. I take another nibble of the cookie as she stays focused on that. It's not long before I clear my throat, and she looks up.

"What?"

"Nothing, just still very upset about last night."

Just remembering how Garrett tried to reach out *again* makes my body shudder. Willow and Luisa were there right when he texted. After a few glasses of wine, I explained our history.

Her eyes watch me before she rolls them and huffs out a breath. "Are you talking about your ex? I thought he was old news. You deserve so much better than someone trying to reconnect just because they're lonely."

"I know I deserve better. But it doesn't help getting texts from him wanting to talk."

"Then block him."

I look at her, almost opening my mouth to protest, but she *tsks* under her breath before dropping the magazine and reaching a palm out.

"Phone. Now."

"You're kidding," I half-heartedly laugh. But Luisa's expression is anything but comical. She's got her brows raised, her lips pursed, and I can even hear her foot tapping against the hardwood.

I roll my eyes before grabbing my phone from the table, unlocking it, and handing it to her. She smiles happily.

"Thanks, Rose. Now, I'm just going to block him, and you'll be able to forget him forever. He's a thing of the past, and plus... There is *way* better out there. Have you seen the men in our club?"

She's busy tapping the screen as I respond. "Yeah, I know. I'm still hesitant about the whole *trying to meet more members* thing. Reeve was a one-time thing. And the raffle last weekend was too big of a step to take. I need baby steps."

Luisa hands me back my phone, and I place it face down on the table. She narrows her eyes. "Reeve doesn't count. You guys casually dated *outside* of the club. The raffle could've been your breaking point."

"I know." I sigh.

"What's holding you back? Are you scared?"

"Slow down with the questions," I say, pressing my fingers against my throbbing temples.

She leans forward, looking at me with more intensity. Her sweet perfume wafts my way, and my stomach twists with nausea. "I'm serious! It feels like this is all we talk about, and you just run around in circles. You deserve to try out what the club has to offer. Seriously, Rose. So what's stopping you?"

I look down at the cookie and already regret it. I suddenly feel like a balloon and want to walk it off and go home. But I can't. Luisa doesn't deserve that. I contemplate even calling Clementine to talk to her, but she's busy with my dad and building the nursery.

Dahlia is already a handful, and I can't imagine preparing for another baby. I don't want to bug them.

"I don't know…" I finally say. But she's not buying it.

And by divine intervention, I see my scapegoat. Or at least a way to direct the conversation to something else. He walks into the cafe, looking around for a moment before locking eyes with me.

"Frankie!" I call over, smiling widely and waving. Luisa whips her head in the direction of my distraction, and she then turns back with widened eyes.

"Shit, he's hot. *Quién es*?"

"Shh! He's coming over!" I swat the air to silence her, and she bites her lip, holding in a laugh.

Frankie gives me a small wave before walking to our table.

There's a vacant chair at the table next to us, so he grabs it and pulls it close. His frame fills the whole seat as he sits down, and his knee bumps into mine.

"Luisa, you're staring," I giggle. Frankie looks at my roommate, and he smiles warmly.

"Nice to finally meet you," he says, raising a hand to shake. She seems transfixed by him, so I nudge her with my foot under the table. That seems to do the trick as she laughs and reaches out, shaking his hand.

"Luisa," she stutters.

"I know. Frankie," he laughs.

Before Luisa could ogle any longer with him noticing, he whips his head to me and gives me a once over.

"What are you wearing?"

I glance down at my shirt with a red wine stain. It's a New Jersey Jaguars shirt. *His* hockey shirt that he accidentally left one night seemed too comfy to keep on the couch. The oversized sweatpants don't help at all with his curiosity. I look like the complete opposite of what Luisa's wearing today.

"A shirt?"

He chuckles, his voice gravelly and thick like honey. The heat in my belly begins to pool, and I *really* hope my cheeks aren't red. "Mine? You're seriously using my shirt to sleep in?"

"How'd you know—" Luisa starts, but I cut her off.

"So?" I glare at Frankie. "It's Tuesday morning. I'm hungover, and I didn't bother to change."

His expression is playful, and he pats my knee under the table. I jolt at the touch, and my cheeks warm. " Of course, Rosita. I didn't mean to offend. Keep it. It looks better on you than it ever will on me."

"Are you living in New York now?" Luisa asks, attempting to reel us back to the table's conversations and popping our little bubble. His hand stays on my knee, and I almost melt. I don't even know if he realizes the effect he has on me.

He shakes his head. "No, just here visiting a friend. Should be going back to Sunny Cove in the next week or two. But it depends."

"On what?" I ask, finally finding my voice.

He glances at me for a moment before looking back at Luisa. "*Cosas.*"

Huh?

Luisa doesn't seem to notice my confusion. She laughs a little too high-pitched for my liking, and she smiles so widely that crinkles appear in the corners of her eyes.

Wait, why am I jealous? She can flirt with him if she wants to. He's single. She's single…

Frankie's hand squeezes my knee and brings me out of my head. I clear my throat and busy my hands with picking apart the cookie in front of me.

"And how do you guys know each other?" Luisa sits back in her chair, glancing between the two of us.

I shrug. "He's my dad's best friend."

Frankie laughs. "*Claro.*"

The next few minutes are back-and-forth questions, mainly Luisa asking Frankie what he does and anything else she can pull out of him. His hand never leaves my knee, only to smooth over my thigh and then back in place.

It creates a swarm of butterflies in my belly and goosebumps all over my body. I'm not sure why he's doing this, but I don't want him to lift his hand just yet.

Luisa finally sighs and looks at her watch. "I've got to go to work soon. Are you sure you'll be okay with that hangover?"

I nod, giving her my best smile. "Yeah, thanks for the cookies. Text me when you're at work."

Frankie sits taller before removing his hand from my knee. "Nice meeting you."

"Likewise," she smiles before turning on her heels and

heading out of the cafe. It's not long before my phone pings, and I see a text from none other than my roommate.

LUISA
Is he single?

ME
Absolutely not a chance. Don't even try.

LUISA
Why not? If you won't have him, why can't I?

ME
He's at least two decades older than us, that's why.

And it'll be weird. He's my dad's best friend.

LUISA
What's that have to do with me? It's not weird

if you haven't known him all your life. Right?

ME
I've only known him since college.

But still, no. End of discussion.

LUISA
Fine. He didn't even show me any interest.

He couldn't stop staring at you. So get on that.

Or bring him to the club.

ME
He cannot know about that.

He'd tell my father.

LUISA
He seems like the type to hide a secret.

And those hands look like they know how to
use rope.

"Everything okay?" Frankie asks, leaning toward me and glancing at my phone. Without another thought, I slam it down on the table, and my cheeks burn.

"Y-yeah! Totally," I mumble, hoping he didn't catch any of that.

His eyes watch me slowly before he smirks. "Are you free tonight?"

"What?" My throat gets tight, and I attempt to swallow, but it's hard.

"Free. Tonight? Or do you work?"

I shake my head. "No."

He raises a brow, and I feel even more dumb in front of him. I glance down at his hands, which are scarred in some places from the machines at work and look like they'd be rough. I haven't stared at his hands this meticulously before. I can't take my eyes off them. And now I can't stop picturing them with rope wrapped around them. *Damn it, Luisa.*

"Hmm? No…" he repeats.

"No, I'm not free. I'm working, sorry, Frankie." I sigh.

"But you're hungover; you need to rest. I can swing by a restaurant and grab some soup. Maybe a grilled cheese?"

My heart warms at the gesture. "Thanks, Frankie, but I'll be fine. I just got wine drunk and kept drinking when I got a text. I'll be fine."

"You said that twice. Are you sure you'll be fine?"

I nod.

He doesn't buy it. "Who texted you?" He leans in a little more, pushing himself into my personal bubble. But I don't mind. His cologne suddenly fills my senses, hints of honey and something musky, and I want to drown in it. Funny how his cologne doesn't bother my hangover state like my roommate's.

I take a deep breath before glancing at his deep, brown eyes. Eyes that are watching me with intent, before gazing down to my lips for a split second. But I catch it.

"No one important." I wish it were Reeve who texted me, to be honest. He's easier to communicate with. He knows when to take my no for an answer. Which makes sense with how he's a noble member at our club. Garrett thinks just because he's reaching out via text that he can continue even when I ghost him.

I silently thank Luisa for blocking him.

"But they're taking up space in your head, Rosalía."

My lips part, loving the way he says my name. He leans in more, his knee pushing up against my thigh to the point where it hurts. But I love it and don't want him to scoot back.

"Not anymore. They're blocked. Done. *Nunca más*."

"Good. I don't want to have to deal with them."

I suck in my breath. "What do you mean, Frankie?"

His eyes flicker to my lips once more, but this time *slower*, so I catch it for sure. As if he *wants* me to catch him in the act. Prey watching the predator devour them with their eyes alone.

Is he doing this on purpose? It feels hotter in this cafe, and I want to fan myself, but I resist it.

"I told you I'll protect what's mine." His voice is low, making me lean in to really listen. He says it with such ferocity that it shakes me to the core. There's no hesitancy in his words.

A gasp leaves my parted lips, and a faint smirk fills his face before going back to a stone expression.

"You don't mean that. Besides, I can't tell you exactly who. You'd just tell my dad."

He cocks his head to the side and stares intently.

"You think I tell your dad everything, Rosalía?"

I gulp and stay silent. I don't know how to respond to that.

He smirks. "There's plenty I haven't told him. There are

some things that just shouldn't be shared with Arlo. I like keeping some things to myself."

"Like what?" I push, knowing I am testing the waters right now. Very choppy, enticing waters.

His pupils enlarge for a moment as he stares at me. The heat in my belly is a full-on fire, and the ache between my legs is unbearable. I need release. It's been too long. Reeve might've satiated me for a while, but there's someone else who's the object of my desire now.

And he's my father's best friend.

"I'll let you know soon enough," is all he says before sitting back in his seat.

My exhale is shaky, and my lips tremble alongside it. Like I was in those chopping waters and drowning, finally surfacing and gasping for air.

I'm *fucked*.

SIX

THE DOOR to River's office is ajar, and I knock gently, waiting for a hum before I enter.

"Come in," she calls.

Her office is quaint but has everything you'd need for an office in a BDSM club. A desk with a computer and some papers on top, walls lined with calendars and whiteboards for her planning and scheduling, and some lounge chairs that are vibrant purple velvet with black satin pillows on top.

Ronan is leaning over her desk as River smiles brightly at him, a mischievous look plastered on her face. Her eyes glance at me once I get close enough, and she quirks a brow. She's got a pen in her hand, her thumb erratically clicking it open and closed.

"You wanted to see me?" I hesitate.

Ronan looks between the two of us, and he whistles lowly.

"I'll leave you to it. Have a good night, River. Radio me in if there's any trouble downstairs."

River nods swiftly. "You got it. Thanks, Ronan."

He closes the door on his way out, and I take a seat before

looking at my boss. She's leaning back in her chair, studying me. I focus on one of the whiteboards with some of the girl's schedules for the month.

"I want you to help me with something," she finally says.

I look at her, and she's still staring intently. Her eyes narrow for a moment.

"Sure, with what?" I respond almost immediately.

"No, Rosalía, I want you first to hear me out. Don't ever agree to anything that you don't know the full extent of."

"Okay," I hesitate.

She clicks her pen a few more times before dropping it and standing up. She rounds her desk before she's in front of me.

"I'd like you to be more active in this club. I see your potential. I see the passion and curiosity in you. Hold onto it and let it guide you."

I don't say anything for a moment as I take in her words. One half of me doesn't know if I'm ready, but the other half wants to teeter on that edge and explore.

"You don't have to say yes immediately, but I'd like you to consider it. Really think about it."

"I don't know if I'm ready for that," I confess. Her eyes seem to soften a little at my confession.

"Like I said, I see the curiosity. I don't want any of my girls to think they're not enough when they are. You're worth the highest prices in this club, Rosalía. Even more."

I slowly smile. "Thanks, boss. You don't have to inflate my ego. I just don't know if I have what it takes to fully immerse myself into all of that. I like working drinks. It lets me get to know the members on a level that doesn't require my mind to think that they'll regret booking a room with me."

My breath is shaky as I finish, and she nods, twisting her lips.

"Okay, then. New objective. Find a new member to get to

know while you're working drinks. Build trust with them. Build *confidence* with them."

"I kind of did with Reeve, and that didn't go anywhere," I remind her.

She laughs. "As I recall, you both convened outside of the club. That's not the same, Rosalía, and you know that. You clearly didn't trust him enough to let yourself let loose inside these walls with him. I want you to find someone that does that for you."

My mind suddenly flashes back to that member the other day. Snakebite. We had small talk, and I've seen him a few more times after our first encounter. But I never really pushed for more than simple *hi*'s and *hello*'s.

"I can do that," I tell her.

She smiles brightly before I stand. She grabs my shoulders and rubs them in a soothing way, like my dad or mom does.

"You're so beautiful, Rosalía," she starts. "And I'd like for all my girls to know that. To *feel* that."

I nod. "Yes, boss."

"I expect some kind of report the next time you're here, okay?"

"You got it."

She steps back and returns to her desk while I give her one last smile before heading out of the office. I take a shaky breath and head to the locker room to change. I put on the same garter again and pray to whatever gods that Snakebite will be out on the floor so I can give River some kind of report.

Even if I don't really talk to him, at least I can tell her I tried.

❦

TONIGHT IS BUSIER than usual for a weeknight. Members pass through the floor to get to private rooms, and practically every seat is full. Almost every member's wrist is decorated with colored bracelets and charms. On nights like these, Evan is busy prepping glasses of water for our members and restocking anything he needs to.

My feet are sore already from working two hours before I take a seat at the bar and take a deep breath. Evan walks over with a water and passes it to me. I thank him with a nod before chugging it.

"What's going on tonight? Why are we so busy?" I finally ask.

Evan shrugs. "Might be some big money makers that River invited to show them the club. Gotta always have a backup plan for when the richest members end up leaving."

"You really think they'd leave *this*?" I joke, nodding my head to the main floor. Evan chuckles.

"You'd be surprised. We had one of our wealthiest members leave after ten years. This was before you started. He still leaves donations and wires money for the raffles, but it's different when he's not physically here anymore."

"Wow, I didn't know that."

"It's okay. River knows what she's doing to keep us afloat. I heard that she and Ronan have been trying to up the security, too."

"Yeah?" I ask, turning my back to where the security men are flanked on the sides of the club. Ronan is nowhere to be found, so he's probably upstairs.

"It's hard to find loyal security that won't tarnish the name of the club for the sake of the bar upstairs." He points to the ceiling where *Blackbird Silhouettes* is.

"I'm sure they have a veto process just like we do for guests of our members. We could charge them an arm and a leg to join for their travels, but we veto them in other ways," I remind him.

That's what I remember hearing from the other girls, at least. If a member has a friend they'd like to bring to the club, they have to go through background checks, verify their bank statements, employment, and anything else that allows River to know that they won't jeopardize our lives and the club.

"No more security talk. How are you feeling tonight?" he asks with sincerity. There seems to be a lull in the water orders, so he stations himself in front of me across the bar. He's got some sweat on his forehead, causing his baby hairs to curl into their natural form.

"I'm doing better, had a talk with River. She wants me to try more out there," I say, throwing my thumb back at the main floor.

Evan smiles. "And are you going to? Or are you going to keep sending out my drink orders when we *all* know that's not something you want to do the rest of your time here?"

My hands lift to my mask, and I adjust it a little before I grasp the empty water glass. The condensation creeps into my palms, and I watch him.

"Well?" he pushes.

"I want to. But I want to find someone I feel confident enough around. Someone I can fully trust," I say, mimicking River's words but in my own way. I don't even think that's what River wants me to do. I own it and make it my choice.

Evan's eyes flick to one side of the club before landing back on mine. He raises a brow and smiles like a Cheshire Cat.

"Tone down the creepy Purge smile," I laugh.

He presses his lips together. "Your new favorite member has arrived."

My heart picks up a little at that, and I hate how I know who Evan is talking about. *Snakebite*. I swivel around in the stool and set my eyes on the man walking to a vacant chair. His eyes roam the club before hitting the bar and finding me. My face burns, but thank god for this mask.

He gives me a slight wave, and I give him an awkward one back. He doesn't wave over any other girl walking around. He keeps his gaze on mine even after he sits.

"Get his order. He clearly wants you to serve him tonight." Evan is loud behind me, and I snap my neck to him.

"He'll have a water," I say without a second thought. *Woah, I'm really trying to get him to a room. Slow down, Rosalía.*

"Atta girl," Evan smiles as he starts to fill a glass with water. In seconds, I've got the glass in my hand, and I'm making my way to Snakebite.

"Here, sir, your drink," I say, bending to hand him the icy drink. Like all the other times he's done, he rakes my figure for a moment, and I melt under his gaze. He doesn't seem to argue with the choice of water, and I quickly glance down to see that he's got a rose gold bracelet now. There aren't any charms yet, but that's a step.

It feels like we're both teetering toward the idea of wanting to do more in this club. It brings almost a sense of comfort to me in a weird way. I don't even know the guy, yet here I am, glad he's taking baby steps like I am.

"*Gracias, Ángel.*" His eyes don't leave mine, and I know this is my chance.

Do it, before you regret it.

I clear my throat and squat to really get eye-level with him, but he's pretty tall. I grip the arm of his chair for balance.

"*De nada,*" I answer and his eyes seem to light up from the Spanish response. Like he wasn't expecting me to understand what he just said. "Are you staying here for a while?" I ask, attempting to bat my lashes at him. *God, I suck at this. It was so easy with Reeve.*

"As long as the night lets me," he responds with a gruff tone that instantly creates goosebumps on my skin. A good kind of shiver runs down my spine.

I giggle and lean in closer. His brown eyes are fixated on

mine through his mask. "I meant after. I've seen you around more than a few times, so I want to know if you're here for good."

He chuckles lowly. "Still figuring that out. I might, I might not."

I stare at him for a moment with his answer. He doesn't know if he's staying here? God, why is this so hard?! *Just ask him to go to a room, Rosie.*

I look around the club and see all my friends with their regulars, and I envy them. I don't really have any regulars, as much as Ronan jokes upstairs.

"Hey," Snakebite says, causing me to look back at him. He shifts in his seat and leans closer to me, his cologne invading my senses. I breathe him in like air, like I won't ever be able to breathe on my own without him.

"Yes, sir?" I ask, watching his eyes as I say that word. He likes it.

"I'd like to be honest with you," he starts. I widen my eyes and bite my lip. Fuck, he's married. He's got a family. He's not supposed to be here.

My mind runs a mile a minute at what he could say. He reaches out and touches my hand, and it sends a jolt of sparks up my arm. I gasp, looking at him.

"*Lo siento,*" he whispers. "You just looked like you were running a marathon in those pretty eyes. You okay?"

I nod. "Of course, sir."

His lips curl into a smile before he lifts his hand, and I immediately miss his touch. Something about it is so comforting and so *natural*. But also something I can't quite put my finger on.

Familiar?

I try to clear that from my mind as I focus back on the very handsome member in front of me.

"I'm obviously new here," he clears his throat. "I don't know how much longer I'll be here. Could be days... could be months."

"Okay," I respond, waiting for more.

"I've got a friend here that vetoed me in. So, I'm new to all of this. I don't want to say or do anything that will make you feel pressured. But I've really enjoyed just our small talk so far these last few times I've been here."

I smile, my body relaxing instantly. "I've got to be honest with you as well then," I tell him. His eyes widen a little and I can almost imagine him raising a brow under that mask. I watch his lips press into a thin line before nibbling on them.

They look like very good lips. Kissable lips. In more ways than just kissing mine. I'd like him to kiss me all over.

"Go on," he urges.

I look around the club and lock eyes quickly with Evan at the bar. He nods at me in a reassuring way. I stand up, and Snakebite looks up at me from his seat. I reach my hand out, shaking a little at the confidence I'm trying to exude.

He takes it, and his hands are calloused. Rough. Like a hard-working man. Very different from a lot of these members I've shook hands with that have very soft hands.

In a way, it reminds me of my father, who worked so much that he had permanent calluses on his hands.

Stop thinking about your dad, Rosie.

"How about we find a private room just to talk? No pressure for anything right now, especially given your lack of charms on that bracelet," I suggest.

If I want to start building trust with a member, I can't just get in one of the kink rooms with them. I have to abide by their decisions, what their bracelet tells me, and be vocal about what I want as well. I want to build trust so I know that nothing will go wrong. If he's fine with this suggestion, then I know he'll be a good contender.

He stands up, making me crane my neck to look up at him. His hand squeezes mine.

"Lead the way, *Ángel*," he whispers.

I don't let my mind wander and hesitate for a second. My feet are already making their way to the side of the club, which has private areas with heavy black curtains to block out anyone else.

SEVEN

IT SEEMS to be like another world behind these curtains. There's a loveseat on one end of the wall and then an L-shaped booth with a table on the other wall. The curtains are the only thing separating us from the rest of the club.

"Sit," I say to him, pointing to the loveseat.

"Yes, ma'am," he chuckles, and it doesn't do me any good.

I want to jump his bones, and I have to control myself. What the hell is going on with me?

He sits on the loveseat, almost taking up the damn cushion before he scoots over a little to allow me to sit. I take a seat gingerly and play with my hair for a moment, nerves suddenly taking over.

There's a moment where he's lifting a hand to his mask, and I gasp, raising my hands.

"You don't have to take it off, not right now," I tell him.

He looks at me for a moment before he scratches underneath the mask. *Oh.*

"Wasn't planning to do that so early on," he laughs. He places an arm over the back of the loveseat, and his hand is over my shoulder. I lean into it and watch his eyes watch me.

My heartbeat increases by the second, and I'm not sure if I'll survive even this private small talk.

Get to it! The devil on my shoulder screams at me.

"So," we both say at the same time. I zip my lips and smile, holding back a laugh.

He clears his throat and flashes his smile. "What's your name? I never got it. And I didn't want to bother any of the other girls with it. Not even sure if they'd give me the real one or a nickname, which I don't mind at all. But calling you over with a name you don't recognize would be rather awkward." He rambles for a little before I giggle.

"It's fine. And yeah, with members, I've found that a nick-name helps before we really get to know each other. I've had—" I almost start to mention Reeve, but I stop myself. Snakebite gives me a look of curiosity before I shake my head and continue, "I let members call me Rosemary."

"Like the seasoning?" It's a genuine question on his part, but nonetheless, it makes me giggle again.

"Yes. Like the *plant*."

He nods. "Rosemary," he says out loud and slowly. For some damn reason, that makes my skin prickle up in goosebumps.

Holy shit.

"Yours? Or what would you like me to call you? I've got one nickname already, though."

His eyes widen for a moment before he chuckles. "*Dime*."

I bite my lip for a moment before I smile and lean in closer. He does the same. His brown eyes are studying me. And not just my own eyes. But my whole face. His stare makes my whole body burn, and I inch a little closer on the loveseat until my knees brush up against his thigh.

"Snakebite," I finally breathe out.

He looks stunned for a moment before he looks up at the ceiling and then laughs. "Because of my drink?"

I nod. "That's what I usually do if I don't get a member's

name. I just call them their drink order. Or their seat number for the night."

He watches me explain, and there's a smile that reaches his eyes. "I'm glad I stayed long enough to get to know your name, even if it's not your real one."

My cheeks warm and it's harder to take my next breath.

"So, your name?" I ask.

He's quiet for a moment, and my chest tightens. Am I doing something wrong? Does he regret being in this room with me? Is this outfit not right? I knew I should've eaten less this morning or went for a walk. I was so busy with—

"I kind of like snakebite now that I'm thinking about it." He interrupts my racing thoughts, and I look at him, amused.

"Really?"

He nods and smiles, leaning in a little more and brushing his thumb over my shoulder. It's delicate, and I want him touching me all night.

"Well, then. I'll call you that." My eyes don't leave his until he's pulling back to relax on the couch.

A hint of doubt fills my brain, but I push it aside. Small talk was much easier outside on the main floor, where there were distractions and things for me to look at. In this small space, there's only *him* to look at.

He watches me for a moment, and I study the mask that adorns his face. I trace the pattern with my eyes, and he seems to do the same until his gaze falls on my outfit and the garter I've come to really like wearing. Around him, specifically.

"This," he says, leaning over and hovering a hand over the garter. He lifts his gaze to mine, and I nod.

He presses his palm over my thigh. His hand is so huge it practically engulfs my thigh, causing a shiver to run down my body. I practically melt under his touch. His fingers play with the garter for a moment, and I hold my breath.

"So, what might make you stay... or leave?" I push out, exhaling loudly.

He doesn't stop playing with the garter when he looks up at me through long lashes. We're inches apart, but I want to be nose to nose. I lean in a little and rest my arm over his on the back of the loveseat. I let my fingers play with the fabric of his dress shirt. Let my hand run over the smooth ridges of the muscles underneath. I revel in the feel of *him* even though I don't even know who this stranger is.

"Do you want the unvarnished truth?" he whispers.

I nod a little too eagerly, and he chuckles before continuing, "I've got some meetings with clients that may or may not end well."

"What do you mean?" I ask, looking at him intensely.

His fingers fumble a little more with the garter. "If they want me to work for them, then that's great. But I've got a life in another city. I'm not so sure if I can leave that all behind."

He's not looking at me anymore. He's keeping his gaze focused on where his hand is, and I can tell he's lost in his thoughts.

"It would be temporary, right?"

He shrugs and continues to focus on the garter. "Yeah, it could very well be. But I've never lived outside of my home-town. I travel a lot, but living in another city—let alone New York City—would be new for me."

"It's not as scary as it seems," I assure him. I think back to my transition from living in Sunny Cove to New York City. It was hard but manageable. It made me grow thicker skin, and I learned a lot about myself.

"Yeah? Are you from a different town, too?" He seems genuinely interested and looks at me like I'm a lifeline. Like the next few words will make or break him.

It's just occurred to me now that we're having such a vulnerable conversation. We're not doing small talk anymore. It's like he's waiting on advice for a huge life-altering decision. *No pressure.*

I nod. "Yeah, a few states away, actually."

"Hmm," he says softly.

"It was a hard time at first," I admit. "But I really like living here. I knew I wanted more than just some small-town life where everyone knew everybody. I like going out into the city and meeting new faces every day."

He smiles sheepishly. "You sound just like someone I know."

"Yeah?" I watch him deep in thought. Is he talking about an ex?

"Yeah," he whispers. "Small town, moved to a big city. But she seems to be thriving, and I envy that."

"Does she happen to be in this city?" I ask slowly. I'm not sure why I'm starting to feel a hint of jealousy. Maybe he's trying to get over her and came here with his friend to take his mind off her?

My mind continues to think about the possible scenarios when he snaps the garter on my thigh, and I squeal, moving my free hand over his and pressing his palm down.

"What was that for!?" I ask, watching as his eyes turn from curious to amused.

"Just wanted to bring you back to this room. You seemed to be elsewhere."

I bite my lip and shrug. "Can't help it."

He digs his fingers into my thigh for a moment, causing indents, and I revel in the feeling. I release my grip on his hand before looking back at him.

"It just seems so odd for me," he continues. "I'm forty years old and terrified of moving to a new city for a few months. Is that crazy?"

I shake my head. "Not at all. My family has lived in the same town all their life. My mom moved out a few years ago. She was terrified, but it was the best for her."

I'm not sure why I just delved into that part of my life with this stranger. But his aura feels secure, like I could trust him with this information.

"Hmm," he murmurs. "But it's also freaking me out that I want that chance."

"To live here?"

He nods. "Yeah. Everything in me is screaming that this is the right thing to do. The right step for my future. But how can I leave everyone behind?"

"Sometimes you have to rip the bandaid off. It'll sting, but they'll understand. Plus, you deserve to do this for yourself, right?"

He takes my words slowly and then gazes at my lips. "Yeah, you're right." He then looks at his watch before cursing under his breath.

"You have to go?" I ask, releasing my arm from his on the back of the loveseat. He rubs the garter once more before lifting his hand. I miss his touch almost instantly.

"Yeah, I've got a meeting with that client in an hour."

"This late at night?" I raise a brow.

He chuckles. "Would you be surprised that one of the possible clients is from *this* club? We're meeting at the bar upstairs."

My thoughts go to Reeve instantly. My smile drops. "No, I didn't expect that."

I can feel my mood change. I don't really *care* if the client of his might be Reeve, but I want to move on from him. I want to find someone with no ties to my previous partner. But I don't think it would make any sense to Snakebite if I explained that. It seems too childish and too outlandish to get to this conclusion.

"I really enjoyed this tonight, Rosemary," he says before standing. I get up as well, and he's adjusting his mask and rolling down his sleeves. He's struggling a little to rebutton them at the cuffs, so I help.

"Here, I've got them," I whisper before buttoning the two on one side and then the other two on his other wrist.

We lock eyes once I'm done, and he's silent for a moment.

"*Gracias, Ángel.*"

"*De nada*, sir," I say before his pupils seem to enlarge. I take a step back to let him leave the space.

He gives me one more look before moving the curtain, and the club music instantly fills the space. I jump a little at the sudden noise, forgetting where I am.

"You coming?" he asks, holding onto the curtain for me to pass.

I nod. "Yeah, thank you."

We walk out of the area, and he's instantly putting his hand on the small of my back as we make our way to the front of the club. I glance quickly at the bar where Evan is, and he's already staring, lifting his hands to give me a little clap. I roll my eyes and laugh.

Once we're near the entrance that leads back to the bar upstairs, he turns to look at me. It feels like the bubble we've been in the last hour has popped, and I'm back to reality. Back to being Rosalía and having to dodge River's order to be more active in the club.

But at least I did a private curtain room with a member. She'd eat that up.

"So," he starts. "I'll see you around?"

I smile. "Sure, Snakebite."

"Is it weird to ask the next night you'll be working?" He plays with the collar of his dress shirt. He seems nervous.

I reach for his arm and rub it as softly as I can. He seems to relax with that. "I'll be here in two days. You'll do amazing with the client, I'm sure. Go secure that future in NYC."

My tone is joking, but I'm serious. I like talking to him, and I hope he stays for a little longer. Even if it's a few more weeks.

He smiles before reaching for my chin, and I instantly still. But I don't step back or slap his hand away. His touch is soft and so, so warm. I want more. His thumb caresses my cheek before lingering close to my lip.

"Thanks, *Ángel*. I'll report back in two days," he smiles.

Without another second, he turns and disappears down the hallway that leads to the stairs.

I feel dumbstruck and frozen in place before another song kicks into the speakers, louder than the last. It jolts me out of place, and I press my lips together. I walk back to the bar where Evan is eagerly waiting.

"So?" His brows wiggle while he's flashing a bright smile.

"He's nice," I tell him, hopping on a stool.

"Really? He didn't try to go against all the rules and bone you right there?" Evan jokes. He knows that security would've been all over that if it did happen.

"He'll be back for my next shift," I blurt. My cheeks warm, and Evan catches it.

"He's dreamy, and you're dreamy. The perfect *dreamy* match," he almost sing-songs.

I roll my eyes. "Shut up."

"Just accept the compliment, or I'll talk to River."

I gawk and lean over to slap his arm. "You wouldn't!"

"No, but you should've seen your face! Now go bring these drinks to the new members that walked in."

Evan points to the tray ready for our members, and he goes back to making new orders. I hop off the stool and grab the tray before heading off to the main floor.

But my mind drifts off to Snakebite the rest of the night. And I hate to admit it, but the thoughts of Frankie slowly dissipate into a cloud of mist.

My thoughts are solely on Snakebite and him alone.

EIGHT

I'M SO FUCKING NERVOUS. My heart keeps racing at the thought of how tonight might go. I see *him* again and don't know what to do with myself. This has never happened before.

Snakebite is the first member that I've taken behind closed curtains. And I want to do more with him.

River would have a field day if she could hear my thoughts. She'd clap her hands and be proud that I'm finally putting myself out there to find a connection with a member.

Even if it is temporary. The feeling of nerves amplifies with the sudden thought that it's not permanent.

He'll either stay here for a few weeks to work out whatever deal he has with his clients or leave. But all the possible scenarios of him staying in New York are temporary.

It's hard to keep composure when all I want to do is see him again.

A sound from across the apartment grabs my attention, and Frankie is busy making us sandwiches. I offered to get us lunch from one of my favorite spots a few blocks away, but he saw how full my fridge was and wanted to make us something.

"*Estás bien?*" I call out from the couch. There's a grunt from the kitchen that doesn't sound good, so I get up and make my way.

He hears my footsteps, and I see him shake his head as I near the kitchen. "No, Rosita, I got this! Sit back down. I swear I remember how to make your dad's sandwich."

I giggle at this, and his eyes lift from the kitchen table to me. He's wearing a tight-fitted blue shirt and some jeans. He looks so ordinary, yet not at all.

Although the last few days, my mind has been on a stranger, some feelings are surfacing when I'm back to being around Frankie. He's been busy the last few days, so I couldn't see him.

"Are you sure? I can text him for the recipe," I say, grabbing my phone from my back pocket. But Frankie beats me to it and leans over, grasping the phone and placing it on the table.

"No, I got this. Trust me," he breathes out.

I hold back more laughter as I watch him scratch his head, make his way back to the fridge, and yank out a few more ingredients. It's a simple sandwich, but I'm guessing he's got something going on he's more focused on.

I see the tomato on the table and grab it, heading to the counter with the cutting board. I begin cutting slices to add them to the sandwiches.

Frankie doesn't seem to notice as he's still rummaging through the fridge. I take a seat and clear my throat. He looks up and sees the missing ingredient he was looking for.

"Oh," he half-heartedly laughs.

I cross my arms and stare at him. "Everything okay?"

He closes the fridge before settling in the chair diagonal from me. Our knees bump, and he presses his lips together before sighing.

"Not exactly. But I don't want to get you worried about me, okay, Rosita?"

The kid nickname still annoys me, but it's for the best. I hold back my own sigh and try to be there for Frankie. "I'm here for you. Is it your friend? Did he kick you out? You can stay on our couch in the meantime. Luisa won't mind."

"She'd love that," he jokes.

"I mean, if you like that, then go ahead," I say, looking at him slowly to see how he reacts to that idea of Luisa. But he pays no mind as he picks up the sandwich and takes a bite. He looks at me and hands me the sandwich, and I take it, biting into it. We share the sandwich for a few more bites before he finally talks.

"I don't want to disappoint your dad."

"How do you mean?"

He shrugs. "I'm out here doing what I can, and he's back there dealing with the rest of our company and Dahlia."

I reach my hand out to hold his wrist, and he looks at me intently. "They'll be fine. You're going back soon, right? You're not gone forever. I love having you here, but you don't have to stay in NYC, right?"

It's been comforting having Frankie so close to me, but if he needs to go back to Sunny Cove to help Dad out with the company, then he needs to do that.

Is he running away from something? Or is he really working here? There are some things I just don't ask him or Dad since it's not my business. But the conversation from a few days ago at the cafe, where Frankie mentioned he could keep secrets from Dad, comes to the forefront of my mind.

"You won't miss me?" He fakes a frown, and I squeeze his hand before retracting and leaning back in my chair.

"Of course I will. But we're busy people. My job is gearing up to add more events closer to the holiday, which means increasing hours to my schedule."

"I do miss Sunny Cove," he adds. "I think Arlo is planning to talk to me soon about expanding and taking over more of the company while he takes a step back."

That wouldn't surprise me. He hasn't told me anything about

that, and Clementine hasn't mentioned it, but it's definitely something that's plausible.

"Well, like I said. If you find yourself staying and need a place, our couch is open."

He smiles and takes the last bite of the sandwich before starting on the other one. I look at the sandwich and already feel like I've gained so much from the few bites I had. The walk this morning was long before Frankie came over, but I want to go for a run.

"Rosalía," Frankie says, breaking me out of my thoughts. I look at him, and his brow is raised.

"Hmm?" I ask.

"I asked if you had to work tonight."

"Oh!" I smile. "Yeah, but can we get dinner tomorrow? I want to show you my favorite Manhattan restaurant."

"It's a date," he says quickly but then freezes for a moment. I do, too.

It doesn't help with the way my stomach flutters. And I'm not sure if it's with nerves or with the way he's looking at me.

"S-sure," I mumble out, breaking out in a sweat and slapping on a smile.

He brushes his hands from any crumbs before standing up. I do, too, and I head back to the couch while he washes the dishes and puts away remnants of our lunch.

Soon after, he joins me, and we waste the rest of the day watching movies and not thinking about Sunny Cove or the future.

Just Rosa and Frankie enjoying their TV time.

HE'S GOT on a dark green dress shirt and black dress pants that fit him perfectly. His mask is a matching dark green, which makes his brown eyes pop. The butterflies in my stomach swarm with intensity.

Snakebite walked into the club with a rose gold bracelet again and no charms.

Baby steps.

He's looking at me from across the private room as I take a seat on the loveseat. I'm wearing, coincidentally, an emerald green corset and matching garter.

"We're matching," I say quickly, settling into the cushion. His eyes rake over my body, and he adjusts on the couch.

"*Pareces un ángel*," he whispers so softly I almost miss it.

My body heats up, and I know I'm blushing bright scarlet under my mask. My hands fidget on the corset ties in the front while I study him and bite my lip. He's got my nerves all over the place. All I could think about the rest of the day after Frankie left was *him*. Snakebite.

"You don't look so bad yourself, Snakebite," I tease. He shifts closer to me on the cushion, and something in me screams to get up. So I do.

I sit up, get on my knees, and press my palms on the cushion before crawling to him.

I have no idea what I'm doing, but I'm doing it.

"Is this okay?" I whisper, watching him for a moment and pausing. He swallows and nods, watching me with doe eyes. No, glazed and hooded eyes. Like he's under a spell.

My spell.

This brings even more confidence for what I do next. My limbs are quick to move as I continue to crawl toward him and latch my palms onto his shoulders. They're strong underneath my touch, and I take a sharp breath.

But I stop to ask for more consent because that's what we prioritize here—consent with each step. Any ounce of doubt means no, and we stop everything until the member tells us to continue.

"Can I sit on you?" The words come out fast from my lips, and he looks almost stunned before he nods, and I straddle him before lowering myself. His hands stay at his sides, and I have to remind myself that most members wait until the employees say it's okay for them to be touched.

"You can hold me," I assure him, and he nods again, lifting his hands to latch them onto my hips. I jolt forward from the feeling as if I've never had a man touch me there before. With this stranger, it feels almost different.

Like I want him to explore every inch of my body. We're in our own little world, and I hope we stay here all night.

His hands smooth over my hips before his fingers press firmly into my skin, causing me to hiss.

"*Carajo, perdón, Ángel*," he whispers, releasing the pressure. I shake my head and grab his wrists, guiding his fingers back to my hips and even moving his hands to a smooth motion. His hands explore my hips and thighs before settling on my mid back.

"We don't have to do anything. If you want to get a charm, though—" I start, but he shakes his head.

"I'm fine like this if you are. We can stop if you'd like."

"Can I be honest with you?" I lean in, causing my core to brush against his growing erection, and I try to steady my breathing. He's definitely *big*.

He swallows and presses his lips firmly together as if he's attempting to regain composure from me accidentally grinding on him.

"*Por supuesto*," he mumbles. I scoot closer until we're stomach to stomach, and my corset rubs against his nice dress shirt. I try not to move too much for the details in my corset to snag on the fabric of his shirt.

I stare at him before continuing. "You're the first member I've ever taken in a private space."

"*En serio?*"

I nod. "Baby steps."

He takes in my response for a moment before smiling. "Baby steps. We go at our own pace. No rush at all, *Ángel*."

The way he calls me angel makes me wonder why he continues to call me that when he knows my 'club' name. But it's not the time to ask or correct him.

"Can I kiss you?" I blurt out, shocked at my own words. But I can't stop staring at his lips.

"*Por favor*," he almost seems to choke out. My hands move from his shoulders to his neck. I glide one hand to caress his jaw before the other grasps the nape of his neck. He doesn't break eye contact while I lean in, his grip on my hips tightening as if he never wants to let me go.

My lips press against his, and they're softer than I imagined. So soft that it elicits a moan out of my lips once we separate. We're mask to mask, his brown eyes boring into mine. The beat of my heart increases, and I roll my hips against him with no caution.

"*Ay, Dios.*"

"Sorry," I mumble, but before I can remove myself from his lap, his hold tightens even more and presses me back into him. My clothed pussy presses down on his erection once more.

He moves a hand from my hip to my cheek before gliding to my neck to pull me in for another kiss. This time is with more intensity, passion, and something else.

Desire.

Like he's starved from a woman's touch and can't believe he got a taste. This fuels a fire in me as I reciprocate the kiss, and his tongue presses against my lips.

"*Puedo?*" he whispers, and I nod quickly so he can get back to it and he pushes his tongue into my mouth.

He groans, and I melt under his touch. Our tongues clash, and my hips continue to circle and grind against him. My body is screaming for more, but I have to remind myself that we're taking it slow. Kissing is all that we *should* do tonight. Plus, he's not wearing any of the flower charms on his bracelet. Although he's able to add them on throughout the night, I'm really hoping he doesn't. I like this. Right here.

He pulls back to stare at me, and I see how red his neck has gotten, and it's traveled up to his cheeks. He's flustered just like I am. His chest moves in rapid motion through his breaths.

"*Estás bien?*" I ask softly, lifting a hand to gingerly brush away a curl of his that moved to the top of the mask. My finger stays on the edge of the mask.

I want to lift it so bad, regardless of my reaction two nights ago when I told him he didn't have to take it off. But I also love the mystery of it all: the ability to stay anonymous in the most vulnerable time.

Because when you think about it, we're drawn to opening up to strangers. It's easier to spill our souls and worries to a stranger than to a loved one. There's no judgment nor expectation to find solutions.

Just two strangers finding solace in each other at the darkest hour.

"I'm fine, *Ángel,*" he responds before pulling me in again. A squeal leaves my lips, and we're kissing again with the same tenacity. The same passion. I'm lost in his lips, and there's nowhere else I'd rather be.

He moans through our kisses while his hands explore my waist and thighs. A hand finds the garter again and snaps it against my skin. I bite his lower lip in retaliation, yet he *growls* under his breath.

And it's the hottest thing I've ever heard from a man. Scratch that. It's the *first* time I've ever heard this coming from a man. And I know I'm already addicted.

Snakebite pulls the garter once more to snap against my skin, and it brings me out of my thoughts of past partners.

"You taste so fucking good," he says in a lower register than what I'm used to hearing. As if that was possible. Like a *true* bedroom voice.

"Less talking, more kissing," I whisper, and he presses my back forward where my breasts in this corset are squished up against his chest. His cologne invades my senses, and there's something so familiar about it.

"Yes, ma'am," he chuckles before we continue our makeout. It feels like we're in this room for hours when I know it has to be maybe half an hour to an hour, realistically.

My lips are bruised and will definitely be obvious tomorrow. His growing beard has rubbed against my skin during our make-out, and I'm sure it'll look like I got a rash in the morning.

But I don't care. The thought of being *marked* like this by Snakebite brings flutters to my core.

The sound of a ringing phone brings us out of our bubble, and he curses under his breath in Spanish.

"*Lo siento, Ángel*," he mumbles. "Swore I turned that off."

"It's okay," I respond, leaning back and watching him run his hand through his hair and pull out his phone. He looks at the screen, blinks his eyes rapidly, and then they turn to concern.

"Everything okay?" I ask.

"Y-yeah, just my boss asking for something."

I take this time to smooth my corset before hopping off him. My shorts are pulled all the way up from my grinding, so I move them back in place.

He's busy texting back before he sighs. "Sorry, didn't mean to interrupt. I know phones aren't supposed to be on."

"It's okay," I lie. It's *not* okay for him to have his phone out in the club just for security purposes and to make sure all rules are being followed. But he seems genuinely sorry, and it looked like an important message.

His eyes flicker to me, and he's still taking deep breaths. "I really enjoyed this."

I nod, playing with my hair out of nerves. "Me too." That's

when I finally remember what we talked about the last time we were here. "Oh! How did your meeting go?"

A smile grows on his face. "You remembered." I nod before he continues. "It went really well. I might have a contract with them for the next few weeks. I've got some more meetings this weekend and next week as well."

"Busy man," I tease, but I'm happy for him for some odd reason.

"This means I get to stay in New York for a little longer, at least." His eye contact doesn't fall from me as if he's gauging my reaction.

I give him a smile, but my heart is stammering against my chest. "That's great! I'm proud of you. See? Baby steps."

"Baby steps," he repeats with a chuckle.

I stand, not wanting to cause anything to get awkward. There seems to be a silence that fills the air, and I don't want him to feel it, either.

He stands, and I have to remember how tall he is. I crane my neck to look up at him, and he lifts a hand to brush a strand of hair away from my mask. His fingers stay behind my ear, and I lose my breath for a second.

"You're absolutely captivating. *Mi mente no puede comprenderlo*."

"Thank you," I let out a shaky breath. *Holy shit*.

"But, baby steps. And I've got a boss to message back. Will you work this weekend?"

That's when his words remind me about our upcoming event this weekend. It's our version of a fun game night that happens once a month.

Members choose however many charms they'd like to try that night and then find a girl to mix in a bowl before she picks one out. It's a roulette of sorts but with our kink rooms. The charm the girl picks is the room they can go to for the night.

If River or any of the girls asked if I was going to participate in this a few weeks ago, I would've said absolutely not. But right now, I want to.

But would he even participate?

"We've got a game night," I start. He looks at me with interest.

"Yeah? What kind of game?" He takes a step closer, creating a bubble around us once more. He's intoxicating.

He's all I can breathe in right now. My mind is like putty.

"Has to do with the charms."

He eyes me before he bites his lower lip. "The charms? Interesting."

"Mhm, so it's not required for you. I know you don't have them on."

He looks down at his wrist with the vine bracelet.

"Will you be working the bar or the game night?"

I hesitate for a moment. It's like whatever I think, he's on the same page too. How is this possible? "I wasn't going to participate. I haven't really participated in any of these events the club hosts. You have to remember that you're the first member I've ever taken into a private space."

"But would you if I did?"

I pause for a moment with his words. He's very upfront about it, and he's saying exactly what I needed him to say as if he can read my mind.

"You'd get some charms?"

He nods, watching me. "Only if you're the girl that I partner with for whatever game the club plans to play."

"Do you want to know?"

He's silent for a moment before responding. "Does it end up with me choosing the charm or the girl choosing?"

"The girl," I smirk.

"Baby steps even with the charms. Right?" He asks softly, inching even closer if that is possible.

"Baby steps, even with the charms," I repeat. "We'll go slow if you'd like."

"I like slow," he whispers. His breath fans over the top of my head. I close my eyes for a moment. Fuck, he's good.

"I like slow, too."

"Tell me you'll participate that night," he urges.

I stare at him with wide eyes. He waits patiently for what feels like a full minute, but I know only five seconds have passed.

"I'll find you that night," I finally say.

"*Perfecto.*"

He nods towards the curtains, and I smile sheepishly, forgetting where we're at once more. The effect he has on me is getting to be too much. I'm unfocused and in another world.

"After you," he says after opening the curtain. I follow him out onto the main floor, letting him press his palm against my small back once more like he did the other night.

Like it fits perfectly and should be there all the time.

NINE

FRANKIE HAS BEEN TALKING to Dad nonstop on the phone while we're walking Central Park. I wouldn't be as annoyed if it wasn't for the fact that Frankie just dropped a bomb on me.

He's going back to Sunny Cove tonight to handle some things with the company for my dad. I thought I'd have him for a few more days before the inevitable.

Frankie groans before ending the call and heading over to me, where I've found a comfy spot on a huge rock a few feet away. We were about to scale these for fun, but he got the call almost half an hour ago. I was so close to getting up to do my own walk, knowing he'd still be on the phone by the time I returned.

"Sorry, Rosita," Frankie says once he's closer. He runs his hand through his hair and huffs out a sigh. "Arlo is already spewing off about twenty things to do on my way back."

"Sorry," I pout. "He's just stressed with Dahlia and Clementine."

She texted me this morning telling me how Dad was *this* close to demoting himself so he could be there for her and

Dahlia. I frantically called him right after but did my best to calm him down and to call Frankie about any business worries.

"Yeah, but he should know that I'll handle it," Frankie spits. He gazes at me and gives an apologetic look. "Sorry."

I shrug. "He wants everything to be perfect by the time the baby comes. He can't let go of either to prioritize one."

"He'll need to," Frankie huffs once more before I stand and grab his shoulders. I shake him for a moment, and he chuckles, glancing down at me.

"Deep breaths, *Tío*," I say, almost regretting that word from slipping from my lips. He pauses for a moment before he chuckles again and grabs my wrists. He brings them to his chest, and we stand like that for a moment.

"Will you be okay while I'm gone?"

I nod. "I've been okay the last year, remember? I'm a big girl. This city is home."

Thoughts of our dinner the other night in Manhattan come to the forefront of my mind. He was such a gentleman, and it felt like a real *date*. Even the damn waiter thought we were celebrating an anniversary. It's so effortless with Frankie, always has been.

He makes me feel like myself and feel comfortable in public, too. I didn't even think about the calories or the damn bloat I got that night from all the food we ate. He even urged me to try bites of dessert, as if he knew I was going through an inner battle with myself about not treating myself to the cake slice.

I want to tell him so bad, he'd understand. I think he'd be the only one besides Clementine who would understand what's been happening lately. Anytime I call her, though, my throat closes up, and I can't say the words. It makes me wonder if this is exactly how she felt before she told me about Nathan.

I need to talk to her though. I know she'd be able to talk me through whatever is plaguing my mind.

Frankie's chest is moving heavily through his breaths, and I twist my palms to press against his coat. He seems to calm from my touch.

"I'll make it up to you," he finally says.

A laugh escapes my lips. "Make it up to me? Why? You were just visiting anyway. I wasn't expecting more."

He shakes his head as if he's trying to make things right. "I know, but I'm a man of my word, and I told you I'd be here for a few more weeks."

"And you're coming back, what's the problem?"

He looks at me while he thinks of a response. His gaze shifts around us before landing back on me. "I'm not sure how well it will go when I'm back in Sunny."

My brows scrunch. "You don't think you'd come back?"

There's a pause, and it's like the whole world has stilled as well. There's no breeze in the air, no birds chirping. But it's most likely my brain trying to focus on his next choice of words.

"I will. Don't worry, Rosita."

The nickname pangs me again. I shift back, and his grip loosens, my hand falling from his chest. I turn to the rocks and start climbing them, continuing to do what we were planning before Dad called him.

"*Con cuidado,*" Frankie calls behind me, and I wave him off. I can hear his steps behind me as I continue to climb the rocks.

There's a moment when I underestimate the gap between the rocks when I jump and miss the rock. I scream and brace for a fall, but strong arms catch my waist.

Frankie pulls me to his chest, and his breath puffs over my head.

"Fuck, that was scary," I whisper, eyes strained on the rock below me that I would've definitely face-planted into. I would've gotten a serious sprained ankle as well, I'm sure.

"I told you to be careful," he chuckles in my ear. I twist my body around to face him, and he's still got me wrapped in his arms. We're inches apart, and I can see some hyperpigmentation on his cheeks, slight freckles adorning his eyes, and crow's feet from years of being his goofy self.

"*Gracias*," I tell him.

We stay like this for a moment, staring at each other, until we hear a sound on the ground near the rocks. Frankie whips his head to the sound, and I do as well. It's a girl waving at us with her phone.

"You guys look absolutely adorable! Can I take a picture and send it to you?!" She's decked out in jogging attire and has some wire buds hanging around her neck. She's already positioning her phone to take a picture.

"Why not?" Frankie calls out, turning back to me. I nod and giggle.

That's when his hold on me tightens, and he does something that even the girl taking the photo couldn't predict.

He leans in, pulling me against his chest tightly and nuzzling his head into my neck. I squirm and squeal as he tickles me, causing my leg to lift and wrap around his thigh. I'm bending my back to attempt to get away, but he holds me tighter, bending with me.

"Frankie!" I scream, feeling his beard scratch my neck, and before I know it, I feel a *bite*. It takes me a moment to realize that he bit my *neck*. Like a goddamn vampire. And it was the hottest thing ever.

He laughs before pulling away and staring at me. I slap his arm before pushing his chest, my own laughter unable to be contained.

"That was such a cute one! Here, let me get a number to text them to." The girl waves us down.

My cheeks burn, and I watch Frankie happily hop down the rocks to the girl. He grabs her phone and enters his number. My hand goes to my neck where he bit me, where it's still warm and slightly wet from his lips and teeth.

The images in my head aren't helping now that he's done this. Why did he do that?

I make my way down the rock, slower to make sure I don't trip like earlier. Once I reach them, the girl is already stuffing her phone in her pocket and grabbing the earbuds.

"You guys are such a cute couple. Have the best day!"

Before we could say anything, she's already jogging away. Frankie and I look at each other before we burst out into a fit of laughter. I slap his arm again, and he takes a step back to dodge it, but I end up slapping his back instead.

"Ow! Rosalía, that hurt!"

I roll my eyes. "No, it didn't! You can take it," I giggle.

His eyes turn to a darker shade of brown I've never seen before as he closes the distance, as if he's ready to banter back.

"You think I can take it? Is that what you think?" His eyes sparkle, and I try to calm down the flutters in my core. The way my panties are starting to get *drenched* from this innuendo conversation.

"Actually, no," I taunt. "No, you can't."

His jaw ticks before he grabs me by the waist. At first, I think he's going just to pull me into a bear hug and suffocate me, but no—he does something *worse*.

He leans down at the perfect moment where I don't realize he's throwing me over his shoulder like a fireman.

"Frankie! Put. Me. Down!"

"Not until you apologize," he mocks, starting to walk the path again. I swivel my head left and right, hitting his back with my fists. People are looking, yet they don't do anything—typical New York City.

If you see something strange, you usually don't involve your-self. It's better not to.

"Francisco Flores! Put me down, *ahora*!" I scream once more, trying to kick my feet, but he's got my knees in a vice grip. A grip much stronger than what I thought was possible.

This newfound realization of Frankie's strength doesn't help the butterflies in my tummy or my drenched panties.

I'm so fucked.

"Nah, uh, need you to learn your lesson," he chastises as he continues to walk, and my head starts to feel slightly dizzy from the blood rushing.

"*Oh*, I'm going to be sick," I groan.

"*En serio?*" Frankie yells before he halts and pulls me back down until I'm standing on my own.

I give him my best mischievous smile before reaching for his stomach and attempting to tickle him.

"Ha! Got ya!" I scream before I turn and make a beeline down the walking path. I have no idea where I'm going, but I can hear his footsteps behind me as he tries to catch up.

"Rosalía!" he calls behind me, but I don't stop. People on the path look at us like we're crazed people, but I feel the most alive.

I burst out into a fit of giggles and out of breath as I slow my run. That's when he finally catches up, and he's leaning over, palms on his knees.

"Out of breath?" I ask, attempting to gain my own.

He looks up from his stance, and his eyes are dark once more. He doesn't say anything; he just continues to stare at me. His cheeks are rosy from the cold and the chase.

He's handsome, and the bite on my neck burns with the memory of what he did.

"I can go all day, baby," he winks before standing tall and wrapping an arm around my shoulders. His grip tightens, and I squeal.

"Too tight, Frankie!" I scream, wrapping my arms around his waist in an attempt to tickle him some more, but he's rigid like a rock.

"No more games, Rosalía," he pants through ragged breaths. "Let's enjoy my last day here before who knows how long."

I look up at him, and he's already staring. I squeeze him harder and bury my head in his chest.

"Want to grab a bite? I know a place with great steaks. And fries."

He nods before loosening his grip around me, and I can wiggle a little more in his hold. But I don't dare let go of his waist. We *do* look like a damn couple in Central Park. That girl was right.

And that idea doesn't leave my mind. It stays with me.

"Sure, you haven't let me down once with your suggestions. I trust you, Rosie—" he pauses before coughing. "Rosalía."

I smile at the name change. "Let's go," I press, forcing our bodies to make a turn at the path where it leads out of the park. The restaurant I want is on the Upper East Side, and we're a few blocks away from there.

"*Vamos,*" he agrees, letting me lead us out of the park.

Without a beat, I loosen my grip once we're on the main sidewalk while waiting for the walking sign. As I take a step away from him, when the walking signal comes on, he grabs my hand from behind.

I look over my shoulder, and he squeezes my hand. I think nothing of it as I keep our hands laced together as we make our way to the restaurant.

TEN

"EVERYTHING OKAY?" I ask Dad once he finally picks up. It's Saturday morning, and Frankie should've been back in Sunny Cove by now. I don't bother to ask Dad, though. I don't want him stressing out any more than he already is.

He sighs over the line. "Yeah, but Clementine isn't doing too good."

I sit up on my couch and stare at the TV screen, watching my reflection. My hair is up in a messy ponytail, and I've still got my pajamas on.

"What's wrong? Do you need me to fly there? She seemed fine on the phone last night."

"She doesn't want to bother you, *mija*."

"But she's not doing well," I remind him.

"No, she's taking this trimester harder than she did with Dahlia. More morning sickness and barely sleeping."

I chew on my lip, thinking of my best friend. I don't know what to say to make him feel better, I just know that pregnancy can be so different each time.

"I'm sorry, but if you need me to fly there, I will. Just say the word."

He chuckles. "*Te amo, mija.* But stay there. I'm trying to be there for her. Work has been kicking my ass lately."

"Language," I giggle.

"*Lo siento, Rosie.*"

"Well, try to be there for her, but also remember that you're not Superman. You can't be at two places at once."

He's silent for a moment. "*Yo se.* I can't do both. Which is why I've been thinking of how to navigate the company."

"Yeah?" I ask, perking up.

He mumbles something before he's coherent. "Yeah, I'm just hoping that it's in the right direction. But enough adult business talk. How's my favorite girl?"

I roll my eyes and laugh. "*Dahlia* is doing just fine."

"Rosie," he chuckles.

"I'm fine, really," I say. "Work is getting busier, so I'll be focused on that for the next few months."

"They pay you well? Benefits? Insurance?"

Typical dad talk. "*Sí, todos.* They take care of me, and I really like working there."

"Good, I'm glad. And Frankie, he's doing okay there?"

I nod, already missing him. "Yeah, I've taken him to all my favorite places around my apartment. I'm hoping to take him to Brooklyn and then Queens later on. I know this spring Luisa wants a trip to the Hamptons, so I'll see if he wants to tag along if he's not busy with the company."

"That'll be nice. I'm sure he'd love that."

"Mhm, maybe Clementine will be okay to visit, too?" I chew on my lip once more.

There's noise on the other line, and he sighs. "Hopefully. She deserves that kind of vacation. I'm glad she was able to go this time to see you."

"Me too," I smile. "Anyway, I don't want to take up any more of your time. Give Clem a hug from me and a big kiss to Dally."

"Will do, *princesa. Te amo.*"

"*Te amo más*," I say before we hang up.

The apartment is quiet this morning as Luisa is still sleeping. I made coffee already, so I plan to let her know once she's awake.

As if on cue, her bedroom door opens, her hair is disheveled, and her pajamas look like she's been tossing around all night. Her eyes are half open when she spots me on the couch.

"Good morning," I say with a bright smile. She squints at me for a moment before smiling.

"*Buenos dias*, is that *cafecito* I smell?"

I nod. "Please, help yourself. I heard you got back home really late last night."

She heads to the kitchen, and I hear her bustling around. Her voice is loud as she answers me. "Yeah, some member wanted the Wisteria room."

I widen my eyes. Wisteria rooms are for wax play. It always intrigued me, but it also felt like it'd *hurt*.

"Really? How was it?"

She emerges back into the living room with a cup of coffee and plops down on the couch next to me. After taking a long sip, she exhales and groans. "Fuck, that's good." She eyes me. "It went really well, but I think I pulled a muscle in my back."

"From the wax?" I raise a brow.

Luisa giggles. "Then another member wanted to go to the Rose room."

Ropes.

"Shit," I whisper. She nods and smirks.

"It was great until I apparently tried to move my arms in a weird way, and that bent my back in a super odd position."

I wince. "You're still going to work tonight?"

"Of course, it's Game Night."

I give her a look as she continues to drink. "You need to rest your back."

She waves me off with her free hand. "I'll just choose a member with either no charms on their bracelet or a very tame room. We're supposed to be making the big bucks tonight."

For some odd fucking reason, my mind drifts to Snakebite. He said he'll take it slow and so he'll most likely have one charm that's a very tame room. Like Bluebell. That's the room where you use blindfolds. Those are usually where new members go to get a feel of the club.

Sudden possessiveness comes over me for Snakebite. I don't want Luisa to see his wrist and assume she can take him. Would he even be able to recognize the two of us besides our hair? Would he even care if another girl took him tonight?

Luisa is looking at me with the mug at her lips. I clear my throat. "I might have someone coming tonight for me."

Her eyes widen. "What?! Really? Is it Frankie? I knew he was into that kinky shit with the way he looks and talked—"

"No!" I cut her off, completely embarrassed. "Not him. Frankie's already back in Sunny Cove for some business. There's someone else that I met at the club."

"No fucking way. It's not Reeve, is it?"

I shake my head. "No, no. Someone new. We haven't even done a room yet, just the private curtain."

"Wow, taking it slow. I love that. And he'll be there tonight?"

"Yeah Even River put me on a mission to get to know a member, so I'm doing that."

She smiles and nudges my shoulder. "That's amazing, look at you! Do you know what room he might pick?"

"Not at all," I say with worry laced in my tone. "What if he suddenly wants to do breath play… or even sensory deprivation? Fuck, I don't think I'm ready for those." I hang my head and bury my face in my hands.

Luisa laughs. "You're choosing the charm, remember? And if he wants to take things fast when you just want slow, then you can say *no*. River will fucking ban the dude if he tries to trick you into one of the more intense rooms."

She's right. I look up at her again. "I know, but I guess it's just nerves talking. I don't even know if he'll show. He could very well be setting me up to be essentially stood up."

Kind of like Frankie and how he should be back in Sunny Cove when I thought I'd be able to distract myself after Snakebite. I was hoping we'd be able to get lunch tomorrow if tonight sucked.

"Don't wrap yourself up with this member. They're nice and have money, but don't rely on them for your happiness. Okay? I don't want to see you hurt over that. They're not worth it if they take your peace of mind away."

I look down at my lap, and Luisa scooches closer on the couch, placing her mug on the coffee table. I don't know how to respond to that. I definitely let Snakebite take my feelings and wrap them in a box with a pretty bow on top. I'm letting him control how I'm feeling, as much as I hate it.

"I just don't want to disappoint him or get disappointed."

She scoffs. "If anything, he'd be the disappointment by not showing. If he can't see that, then it's his loss and you'll move on to the next member. He's not the end all be all, he's simply a transaction. You have to remember that while working."

I lean into her as she pulls me in for a side hug. I rest my head on her shoulder and change the subject. "You don't think I look too bloated in that corset? Or that silk dress I bought the other day? I was hoping to wear the dress and then that sparkly red garter. No tights this time. I want to feel my best."

She's silent for a moment as she takes in my words. "No, not at all. Is that what you're really worried about, babe? How you look?"

Tears brim my eyes, and I don't know why everything seems to be crashing onto me at once.

"I just want to *feel* good enough. Not just for him but for myself."

I don't want to admit to her that since I last saw Frankie, I'm starting to spiral again into deeper waters with my eating disorder. I haven't eaten since last night, and I know I should at least have something in my stomach before tonight.

"You are enough. You're more than enough, and if they can't see it, then fuck them." Luisa squeezes me again.

As if on cue, my stomach growls, and Luisa pulls back. "Let's get something to eat, yeah? My treat."

I look at her for a moment, not wanting to ruin the moment by saying no. But I need to do better. I have to yell at these destructive thoughts that are making me doubt myself. Doubt everything.

I nod slowly. "Sure, that'd be nice."

She pats my knee. "Alright, let's get all dolled up and pretty. And then we can go to work together, okay?"

"Okay," I respond softly. She gets up from the couch and grabs her mug before disappearing into the kitchen. I grab my phone and head to my bedroom to get ready. A shower would do me good. And food. Definitely need some food in me, like Luisa suggested, or else tonight might turn out much differently than what I expect.

Passing out due to lack of food isn't on my agenda for tonight. Work takes a lot of energy out of me, and I can't risk it.

As I get my things ready for the shower, the whole routine shower, I might add, I open my phone and click the text message thread with Frankie. The last message he sent me was from yesterday.

FRANKIE

Here's the photo that jogger took of us. We look great. Especially you, Rosalía.

Attachment: 1 image

I stare at the picture once more. The way my leg is lifted and he's holding my body as we're both leaning toward the rocks. It looks like a damn coordinated couples photoshoot with the way we're holding each other, and he's burying his face into my neck while I'm laughing. We look cute. *Real*.

I haven't responded to the message yet, unsure how to reply to that. My neck tingles like a phantom feeling of where he bit me that day. My stomach flutters with the reminder of what happened.

How I wanted more to happen, but then he had to leave.

It's funny how I'm slowly starting to get to know a member at the club, and then I have moments like *this* with Frankie. My body doesn't seem to know what to do with all these pheromones.

I quickly save the photo into my camera roll, and my fingers work quicker than my brain as it clicks the three dots and then sets the picture as the wallpaper.

My eyes glance over the wallpaper. The photo lights the screen up, and I can't stop staring. The way he's holding me.

What are we doing? We could never be anything.

I shake those thoughts away and head to the bathroom to shower, not wanting to think about the two men anymore. Snakebite and Frankie.

How did I get myself into this position with these two men?

ELEVEN

ANGELIQUE IS DOING my hair again, this time with more curls and some hair tendrils pinned with diamond studded clips on them. The way my hair reflects under the light of the employee lounge is almost blinding.

"Even though your dress is black," Angelique starts, "you look like a damn angel with this hair and that makeup."

"Really?" I fidget my hands on my lap as she continues to finish my hair. She's concentrated on curling one piece while I stare at her in the mirror.

"Mhm," she nods, letting the curled piece fall over my shoulder. "Whoever you choose to do Game Night with will drool. He'll be a truly lucky member tonight."

"You're just saying that," I say hesitantly.

She shakes her head. "Not at all." She makes eye contact in the mirror. "I'm serious, Rosalía. Like a literal angel that has fallen."

"Isn't that a bad thing? Like they've been cast out from heaven and fallen to Earth?"

"The *point* is that he's going to devour you. In more ways than one, I hope." She giggles.

"Maybe. If he has the right charms to choose from. I'm not planning to go into the Magnolia rooms anytime soon."

She smiles before finishing the last strand and then using hairspray all over. I cough a little from the mist before she pats my shoulders.

"All done! Now go get him and tell us all about it next shift."

I turn and hug her, making sure not to ruin the hair she just made. I look in the mirror one last time to see how long my hair has gotten. The dark strands almost touch my butt when I turn around. The black silk dress barely passes my ass, and the red garter seems to glitter even more than the other ones I've worn in the past.

It makes me feel *confident* and *sexy*.

I make sure to check my makeup on my neck once more. The bite Frankie put on my neck wasn't visible by any means, but there were some red marks from it that I wanted to make sure were covered.

"Woah, you look *so* good!" Luisa and Kiki come into the room, and they motion for me to do a twirl like we're in a dressing room trying on dresses.

A giggle leaves me as I finish the twirl, and they clap.

"You should do your hair like that more often," Kiki exclaims.

"Really?" I ask, looking back at the mirror once more. She nods, and so do the other girls in the room who are getting ready.

River is in her office, or else I'm sure she'd also have something to say. She'd probably say, *I told you so*.

Luisa walks over to her chair and pulls something from her bag before heading to me. There's a hair clip in her hands—a beautiful golden clip with diamonds that make the shape of a rose.

"For good luck tonight, my beautiful rose," she whispers.

Tears brim my eyes at her thoughtful gesture and I lean down for her to put the clip in the perfect spot to not disturb the others that Angelique put.

"Thanks, Lu," I whisper, attempting to swallow the thickness in my throat.

"He's going to be out there, and he's going to make it the best Game Night ever," she reassures me before pulling me in for a hug. I breathe in her sweet perfume and whatever else she put in her hair before we pull apart.

"I'll see you out there?" I ask, nodding my head to the hallway that leads out to the club.

She nods. "You bet. Go get him, Rose."

SINCE I'M WORKING the floor tonight and waiting on Snakebite, I don't have the chance to talk to Evan. He's busy at the bar anyway, but I wish I had time to stop by for a chat.

I'm making my way around the huge stage where we'll have River come out to make a speech before the Game Night starts. She loves this themed night so much that she made it a mandatory monthly event.

There's a tap on my shoulder, and I jump, twirling around to be face-to-face with Snakebite. I look up at him, and he's smiling widely. He's wearing another viridian dress shirt, but this time, he's got matching viridian cuff links that sparkle under the lights. His build fits the dress shirt and pants perfectly. His growing beard seems to be a little trimmed down even.

"I'm glad you're here," he murmurs, getting close. I get on my tiptoes in these heels, and I love how he's still taller than me, regardless of the heels.

"Yeah?"

He nods, eyeing my face. "You look astonishing. *Pareces un verdadero ángel esta noche.*"

My lips twist into a smile. "Don't you know that angels shouldn't participate in these kinds of Game Nights?"

"I guess we'll see the punishment for breaking the rules, huh?" His voice is teasing, but the way he says it makes my stomach flutter, and my thong is soon to be fucking drenched.

He looks around the club while they're slowly getting ready for River to get on stage. Members are milling about the bar with their waters, and some are already taking a seat. Then, I see some other regular members with dominants and submissives. Although we have a Game Night tonight, other members who routinely use our rooms are still able to show up.

I see a free chair at the end of the stage, grab his hand, and pull him along. He follows willingly. His calloused hand fits perfectly in mine, and I instantly need him to touch me more.

It's not unusual for a girl to sit with a member in the same chair. And something takes over where I glance at him and nod to the chair. He doesn't hesitate as he takes a seat and pats his thick thighs. I take a deep breath, exhaling all nerves for the night as I take a seat on his thighs, sideways, so one of his large hands holds my ass and the other my knees. The dress rides up incredibly high on my thighs, making it barely an inch or two from my thong peeking through.

The hand on my knees travels a little higher, but not to the point where it's going under my dress. I loop my arm around the back of his neck, and he looks at me expectantly.

"Is this okay?" I ask, leaning in.

He nods and chews on his bottom lip for a little. "*Por supuesto, Ángel.*"

I latch my free hand on his that's found its home on my thigh. Our fingers interlock, and it feels just *right*. My heart is hammering against my chest, and I've got tunnel vision of him.

So much so that I almost miss the sounds of the microphone tapping and River's voice filling the air.

"Good evening, gentlemen and ladies. I hope we're all ready for a great Game Night!" I turn to see River in a stunning red dress that falls to the floor with a slit up her thigh. Her sparkling silver heels show through the gap of her dress as she moves.

The crowd whoops and hollers, and I look around the club for a moment, seeing just how many members are here. It's almost at capacity, and that doesn't shock me.

Game Nights are supposed to be fun, relaxing, and a great way for members to get to know the girls or their partners they bring.

"I've seen some of the Black Silk girls have found their partners," her eyes glance at me for such a short second that I almost miss it. My cheeks warm, and my fingers tighten around Snakebite's. The hand on my ass squeezes it gently as if to calm me. "If you haven't found one yet, be sure to walk around with your charms so the girl of your dreams can choose the best room for you tonight."

She goes on to remind members of the rules that still apply at all times: consent, safe words, and anything else that is mandatory for a sex club. Then she reminds members that if they haven't chosen their charms yet to do that now.

That's when I glance at Snakebite, whose gaze is focused on the stage before looking at me. "Everything okay?" he asks.

"Do you have your charms?"

He nods, unlocking our intertwined fingers to get the charms out of his dress shirt pocket. He's got two.

A rose and kerria.

The charms glisten underneath the club lights, and his palm is huge compared to the small flowers.

"Which one did you want to do the most?" I slowly ask, unsure if he chose these at random or really wants to go to these rooms. All members should know what each flower stands for, but I want to make sure he's ready.

"I thought you were choosing. Isn't that how Game Night goes?" He watches me.

"Yeah," I smile. "But I want to make sure you're ready for these. Rose can get pretty intense."

"So the other? I want to make sure you're comfortable tonight. *Mi preciosa ángel*," he whispers, almost too low for me to catch. I lean in even more until we're nose to nose. I breathe in his cologne, and goosebumps rise on my arms. I instinctively clench my thighs together, and he definitely catches that.

"The other," I whisper.

I don't even register the members around us. I'm stuck in our little bubble once again. He's staring into my soul with his brown eyes, and I want to lift his mask so badly to see who's underneath.

But I have to abide by our rules. Of course, members are allowed to remove masks in the privacy of a room if both parties consent to it. The girls don't have to remove their masks at all, even if the members do theirs. But if I see this man's face, then I want him to see mine too.

"The other then," he agrees. He drops the rose charm back into his pocket and then removes his hand from my ass so he can put the kerria charm on his bracelet. He struggles for a moment before I lean back to assist him. The charm clips on easily.

"*Gracias*," he smirks.

"To the kerria room," I manage to say, even though my body is now full of nerves. I know I'm ready. I really am, but now the thought that I'm actually going into a *room* with someone I've only encountered a few times has my mind going into a frenzy. My nerves are starting to skyrocket.

"Remember, we don't have to do anything if you don't want to," he says as I get off him and stand tall. He stands up and smooths out his dress shirt, his muscles flexing underneath.

I bite my lip. "I know, and you too. You're allowed to back away, don't forget."

He looks at me as he responds. "I'd only back away from you if you ask me to. And I'm really hoping you don't."

The words stumble out of his mouth so effortlessly. My stomach flutters, and it's not nerves anymore, but desire for him.

I reach my hand out, and he takes it as I pull us around the stage. I grip Snakebite's hand a little harder than necessary, but he doesn't seem to mind.

Once we're walking, I finally find Evan's gaze locked on me, and he gives me a small nod and smile. I return it, but my lips are almost shaking from the nerves.

"You okay?" Snakebite whispers, getting closer to me. I give him a nod before continuing to lead us to the hallway with a few Kerria rooms.

I was glad that I could choose a more tame room. The rose room was something I was curious about but not ready for. Ropes and bondage seemed like a room for a more experienced member.

Snakebite and I promised each other to take it slow, and the kerria room seemed to be the best option tonight.

The hallway has a yellow and pink glow for hibiscus, kerria, and sunflower. There are eight rooms down this hallway, each door having a glowing sign of the flower right above.

We reach the first kerria room and I tap the screen near the door for login. All workers have to put in their employee PIN code for safety. River has a tablet and computer that shows which rooms are occupied by which girls, not just for surveillance, but for safety.

One of the golden rules in this club that River makes every worker swear to is never showing members the panic buttons that are stationed in every corner of the club, under chairs, tables, doors, and more. She makes sure that her workers are the safest when locked in a room with a member.

Snakebite seems to understand what I do as he turns away, and I put in my PIN. The screen flashes quickly, asking how many will be in the room. I press two, and then it asks for the member's ID.

"Here, put your ID number," I tell Snakebite. He turns around and looks at the screen before nodding. He's quick to punch in his member ID number. Even though he's a vetted member, he still has a permanent ID with the club.

The screen flashes green, and the door clicks, indicating that it's open. Snakebite pushes the door open, and I make sure the screen works as it transitions from green to red and displays in capital letters *ROOM IN USE: 2*.

The room is dark until Snakebite finds a switch, and the room is flooded with light. I close the door as I enter and then turn the dial for the lights. Mirrors line every wall and even the ceiling.

"Oh," he laughs. "Sorry, I didn't realize you can change the intensity."

I giggle. "It's fine. I don't think anyone uses the highest setting. That would be odd in a room full of mirrors. The reflection would be too blinding."

He seems nervous as he chuckles before looking around the room. He brings his hands to his hips and surveys the place. The authoritative stance makes me stare at him a little longer, wondering what's going through his mind.

He also looks damn attractive with that stance and his formal clothes.

His eyes glance at me, and I blush. "What?"

"Nothing, just a little nervous, to be honest," I confess.

"I am, too, now that we're in here. But remember, if you want to go, we can get out of here."

The suggestion is thoughtful, but I need to rip this off like a bandaid. I *want* to be in this room with Snakebite. No one else. I don't know who else I'd be comfortable around besides him. Not even Reeve, I don't think.

"I want to be here," I finally muster up the courage to say.

He takes a few steps closer to me before taking a deep breath and reaching his hand until a finger brushes under my chin. I gasp, watching his brown eyes take me in. Like he's a man starved, and I'm his last meal on Earth.

"I want to be here too," he whispers.

"Come on then," I say slowly, grabbing his hand and pulling it down from my chin. He looks at the bed near one of the walls. A large dresser at the opposite end of the room is stacked with toys to play with.

But this room, kerria, is meant to be utilized with just the bodies of the workers and members. To explore each other with the use of the mirrors to increase desire and satisfaction.

Katoptronophilia is like voyeurism but with the use of mirrors. There isn't a double-sided mirror with an audience. The worker and member *are* the audience.

I've always thought this room would be one I'd like to try, so I was more than excited that Snakebite had this charm.

The fact he had a rose and then kerria, which is a yellow Japanese rose in his hand. It felt like fate.

"Come on, *Ángel*," he says loudly, breaking me out of my thoughts.

He pulls me toward the bed, and I don't hesitate to follow.

TWELVE

HE'S GOT desire and *hunger* in his eyes.

We're sitting on the bed, my legs practically on his lap while he caresses my face.

"Can I kiss you?" he asks slowly, and I nod, watching the way his pupils dilate as he leans in.

The kiss is softer than the last time, and it feels like my body has been craving for it ever since. The kiss brings me back to life, creating a fire in my body, and I can't think of anything else.

He pushes his tongue into my mouth, and a moan rolls out of mine, causing him to groan and grab my hips harshly.

"*Ah*, fuck," I whisper.

"Sorry," he says as he pulls back with worry in his eyes.

"I didn't say to stop kissing me," I tease before I pull him by the neck to kiss him again. My body works on its own accord as I shift my hips until I'm sitting on him.

Our chests press against one another, and our panting fills the room. The ache between my legs intensifies as I rub myself against him.

"Shit, *por favor*," he whimpers.

I pull back, and he gives me a confused look. "What? Everything okay?"

I smile before placing my hands on his chest. "I never heard that before from a man."

"What?"

"A whimper."

He looks at me before leaning in and biting my bottom lip. I squeal and squirm before lowering my hands on his chest to his sides and tickling him slightly.

"Hey! That's foul play!"

"You're the one that bit me," I protest. His hands on my hips tighten, and I hope they leave bruises in their wake.

"You're delicious. So fucking delicious. I want to bite every part of you," he reasons.

My face heats up at this, and I bite my lip. "Really?"

"*Si, Ángel. Cada parte de ti.*" His hands move from my hips to my waist before climbing higher until they're high under my breasts. He looks at me for a moment, and I give him a single nod. He cups my breasts, and with the V-cut in the center, he uses it to his advantage to squeeze and have them almost spill out of the dress.

His thumbs brush over my covered nipples, and I moan, closing my eyes.

"Oh? You like that?" His voice gets lower, and I feel like I'm about to enter heaven tonight.

"Yes, yes, I do," I pant.

His thumbs then pinch the fabric of the dress, just enough to grab my nipples and pinch them as well.

"Take it off," he says.

I open my eyes and look at him. His eyes seem to shift into a more authoritative glare, and at this moment, if he asked me to get on all fours and crawl to him, I would.

"Yes, sir," I whisper before grabbing the hem of the dress and shifting my body away from his to pull it up and off me. I take care not to knock off my mask in the process. He breathes heavily through his teeth as he watches me toss the dress to the floor.

"*Te pusiste esto para mí esta noche?*"

I nod, running my hands over my lingerie. My nipples are hard and aching to be touched, so I twist them, and it elicits a moan from my lips. His eyes turn dark, and I smirk as he continues to watch me run my hands over the curves of my breasts then down to my stomach.

At first, I thought he'd not be attracted to me once he saw me in lingerie and saw that I'm not all slim waist and skinny. No, he looks at me like he's unable to look away.

He drinks me in.

"Please let me," he whispers, reaching for me. I nod, and he practically falls on the bed as he tries to get to me. His hands are on my laced bra, tracing every pattern and then pulling the fabric down until my breasts pop out. He looks up at me before leaning in and placing his mouth on my nipple.

"*Fuck,*" I whimper as his tongue glides over my nipple, and his mouth sucks perfectly.

I subconsciously roll my hips toward him, and he grabs my waist once more, causing shivers to run down my body. My hands go to his head, grasping his hair, and I yank hard.

"Shit, *Ángel*, be easy on me, please," he seems to beg as he pulls away and looks at me from underneath his lashes.

"Baby steps," I remind him as he nods and latches his mouth on my other nipple. I lean my head back and bite my lip to keep a moan in, but it's no use. It's like a goddamn symphony coming out of my mouth with the way his tongue glides and bites my nipples.

I'm done for, and we haven't even started.

"Please, I need more," I beg, rolling my head back and pulling him off my breast. His lips are shiny with saliva, and he looks almost saddened by what I just did.

"What do you need? *Dime*," he almost pleads.

I look at the mirror to the left of us and see how close the edge of the bed is. An idea sparks.

"The mirror, we should use them, no?"

He looks at the mirror as well, and we lock eyes on it. "Do you trust me?" he finally says.

I nod before watching him get off the bed and then unbutton his dress shirt. He undoes the belt of his dress pants next before placing it on the bed. The sound of his shoes being taken off is next. He then pulls down his pants until he's just in his black boxers. My jaw falls as I study him.

He's not just handsome but *ripped*. Like whatever he does for work daily is lifting heavy things. He's got veins on his arms, and his chest puffs out with muscle, and he's got a six-pack *at least*. The v that points straight to his cock is barely covered by the waistband of his boxers. There's some hair on his chest that travels low, a definite happy trail that sparks something inside me.

He's so *manly*. More than I've ever seen in my life. He takes care of himself, and it shows.

"I'm guessing you like what you see," he smirks at me through the mirror. I look at myself and find my neck and chest slightly rosy from my blushing, and I can't imagine what my cheeks look like under this mask. My brown eyes stare back at me, and I try to calm my breathing.

When he makes a move, my eyes are on him again. He grabs the belt before climbing the bed and getting closer to me. I'm sitting on my knees, watching him with curious eyes.

"Can I wrap your arms with this?" he's right behind me, still talking to me through the mirror. He lifts the belt and waves it so I can see. I nod, unsure how to respond coherently.

Then I remember that he can't proceed unless I verbally consent. "Y-yes," I manage to squeak out.

He smiles before adjusting himself to be pressed against my

back. He grabs one of my arms, twisting it behind my back. I mimic the movement with my other arm until he's got both my arms stacked on one another behind me. At first, I think he's just going to tie my wrists together with the belt, but I feel the way he wraps it around my *forearms*.

"Tight enough?" he leans in and whispers.

"Yes, it's good," I answer, attempting to wiggle out of the hold, but it's no use. My arms are securely fastened together with the belt.

My core flutters, and I clench my thighs. *Fuck*, we're really doing this.

"Now what?" I whisper, almost too excited to know what he's got in mind.

"Can I explore?"

I stare at him through the mirror and nod. He takes his time to lean into me. His chest is warm against my back, and his hands travel from my shoulders to my breasts again. I instinctively lean against him and roll my hips.

"You feel so soft, like a real damn angel," he says as his hands travel lower to my stomach and then my hips. He squeezes my skin, and I almost lose my breath.

"*Please*," I whisper, my hands attempting to reach for anything behind me. Being bound this way and wanting him to touch me everywhere is almost making it that much more *sensitive*. My nipples pebble again, and it takes him no time to notice. His hands are on my nipples in an instant, twisting them between his thumb and index fingers.

"*Ah*," I whimper, pressing my ass against him in retaliation and closing my eyes. He presses his core into me, and that's when my eyes pop open, and I stare at him through the mirror, and he's smirking.

His erection is poking my back, and I've never wanted a man so *desperately* before.

"You're doing okay? You remember the safe words?" he

speaks up, twisting my nipples again before traveling back down to the waistband of my thong. One of his hands moves to my ass and squeezes it.

I squirm underneath his touch and nod, leaning my head back. He leans in, and his lips brush my neck, peppering me with kisses. "I need to hear you say it," he reminds me.

"I'm doing amazing, please, *more*." My body is on fire for him and I don't know how else I can go on. I roll my hips again, and that causes his fingers to slip underneath the waistband. I moan, and he bites my neck.

He continues to suck on my neck and lather me with kisses as I get lost in the moment and continue to grind him this way and that. His fingers finally stop once they're completely underneath the fabric of my thong.

"May I?" he asks, breathing heavily in my ear. He sounds just as desperate as me.

"Please," I lean even more against his chest, and my arms are starting to hurt from how much I'm trying to resist the bondage and break free out of pure desire.

His fingers reach down and lightly touch my clit, causing my body to jolt. "Oh my god," I whimper.

"I haven't even touched you yet," he chuckles.

He continues to explore as his finger rubs against my clit and then lowers to glide between my pussy. I'm so wet, and he knows it. He groans in my ear before biting my neck again and lowering to my shoulder.

"So fucking wet. For me?" When I don't respond, he flicks my clit with his fingers and I scream.

"Y-yes, for you," I whimper.

"*Que linda*, just for me," he chuckles lowly. It sends vibrations through my body, and that causes me to get even wetter, and he's not even inside me yet. But I need him to be.

His fingers glide up and down before his thumb rubs smooth circles over my clit. I'm slowly getting closer to release, at just this, and it feels so pathetic but so *good*. I've never had a man make me come this quickly. Reeve was a close call, but for some reason... *this man*. He knows how to work my body just right with a feather touch.

"I need you," I say, rolling my hips and jutting them forward to cause his fingers to slip lower to my entrance. "Inside me," I finish with a pant.

"So fucking eager for me, baby," he whispers before finally giving me what I want. He slips his thick finger inside me and doesn't do it slowly. He does it in one swoop motion until he's knuckle-deep. It stretches me, and I whine, throwing my head back even harder against him. My arms are starting to feel numb, but I don't care.

"Please, don't stop," I breathe out.

"Wasn't planning on it," he responds as he pumps his finger in and out of me. The sounds of how wet I am fills the room, and my pussy practically swallows his finger with every movement. He slowly enters a second finger before working that in and out of me as well.

"*Tan buena*," he compliments me, and it fills my head with the sweetest praise.

"All for you," I whimper.

"For me?" he asks, and I nod, turning to look at him. Not through the mirror, but face to face. He turns to catch me in a kiss, and he adds a third finger, causing me to scream into his mouth. Our masks clash against one another, making it more of an annoyance that they're in the way when I'm feeling so good and almost to my peak.

I roll my hips to the rhythm of him finger fucking me, and I squirm before pulling away from his mouth to gasp.

"I'm s-so close," I whimper. I shut my eyes tightly, chasing that relief. I'm at the highest point of my orgasm, and I'm about to crash.

Until he pulls his fingers out of me, and I whip my eyes open and stare at the mirror.

"I can't let you come just yet," he says with a shake of his head. I watch as he lifts his drenched fingers with my juices to his mouth before he licks them one by one. My chest is heaving as I watch him for a moment until my body is able to calm down from almost reaching an orgasm.

"Why?" I fairly ask, pouting. He steps back for a moment, and I frown, thinking he might be done with the room. He's over it, and he didn't get as much of a high as I did, and now he's bored.

My mind starts to overthink until he's latching his hands on my arms and undoing the belt. It takes a moment for me to realize that my arms are free to move until I roll my shoulders and flex my arms in front of me.

"Get on your back," he demands as he tosses the belt to the ground. I don't hesitate to flip over and catch my reflection on the ceiling mirror. He leans down to my waist, and I watch as his back muscles flex. My legs wrap around him, locking him in, and he chuckles.

He grabs my legs and kisses the inside of my thighs, and I squirm underneath, giggling. "Oh! I'm so ticklish there!"

"Yeah? Good to know," he says before biting the inside of my thigh, and I squeeze my legs together over his neck. He hisses and taps my thighs, and I release the hold.

"Sorry," I mumble, but he shakes his head.

"I want you satisfied before you choke me," he jokes.

"Okay," I mumble, biting my lip. I look down and watch him lift his gaze to me. His hair flops a little over the mask, and it's the prettiest sight. His lips are still glistening of me, and I buck my hips toward him.

"Let's take this off," he says, nods to my bra, and I oblige, unclasping the bra in the back and tossing it to who knows where. My nipples are still hard, and he admires the sight.

"I'm ready," I tell him, even though I have no idea what I'm in for.

He smiles before kissing my thighs again and then looking back at me. His eyes suddenly turn to mischief. He grabs the sides of the thong before pulling *hard* and ripping it into pieces to give him full access.

"I want you to look at that mirror above. Don't you dare take your eyes off it. I want you to watch yourself come undone as I eat you out. Got it?"

I nod before laying my head back and staring at his back muscles flex as he grips my thighs in a possessive manner. I jolt and moan as he starts kissing my thighs and making his way to my pussy.

His breath fans over my clit, and I whine, doing my best not to look down. I take this time to reach down and grab his hair. It's soft and my fingers glide through effortlessly.

"Good, hold on, baby," he whispers before he glides his tongue over my clit. I whimper and buck my hips at the movement.

He's *good* as he glides his tongue down my pussy and then teases my entrance. He then moves back up to suck on my clit and then continues to glide up and down before pushing his tongue into me. It feels so fucking good, and my lips purse before my brows pinch together. I'm so focused on myself that I start to realize how fucking *amazing* this is. Watching yourself come undone under someone's doing.

"*God*, I can't," I whimper.

"He's not here right now, just me. Deep breaths, baby," he responds before diving back in and pushing his tongue into me. I scream before clutching his scalp even more, and he presses his mouth against my pussy even more.

His muscles are working overtime as he holds onto me, imprinting every inch of me with his fingers. I watch in the mirror as his arm reaches up to find my nipple and twists it, elevating my senses and causing me to grind my pussy against his face.

There's a pinching feeling, and I yelp, looking down and realizing that his mask got caught and pinched my inner thigh.

"Fuck," he lifts his head, wiping his mouth. "Sorry, still not used to these masks."

I push myself up on my elbows, and my whole body moves with my breathing as I try to calm it after his mouth had me go to heaven. "We don't need them in here. We can take them off."

He looks taken back for a moment before remembering the rules. "I forgot. But I respect your privacy and don't want you feeling uncomfortable."

I shake my head, feeling more confident than ever before. "I trust you," I finally say.

This seems to work because he lifts his hand to his mask, but then he pauses and looks at me.

He's nervous.

"What?"

"I don't want you disappointed," he whispers. His fingers hover under the lining of the mask, battling the uncertainty of what will happen once he takes it off.

That's when I decide to take action. I need him to trust me. I trust him right now, and he knows that. But maybe taking off my mask *first* will show him that he can trust me to do the same.

I know it's risky, but that's why this club has so many rules. If he ends up hating me and wants a different girl, then he's allowed to request it. I don't ever have to get a room with him again if that's what he wants.

"I'll go first," I suggest, reaching for the ties on the back of my head.

His eyes widen. "Are you sure?"

I nod. "Yes. Then we can continue, right?"

"No more pinching, that'll be helpful," he jokes. I laugh and then undo the ties with one hand as I continue to steady myself on my other elbow.

He watches carefully, his hands on my thighs. He looks like a kid waiting for the reveal of Santa or something. It's adorable.

I close my eyes as the ties fall and grab the mask, lifting it off my face. I open my eyes and toss the mask to the bed before gazing back at Snakebite.

But he's no longer looking at me with curiosity. His eyes widen in absolute horror, and he wipes his mouth as if he just took the worst shot of vodka in his life.

"Rosalía?!" he screams, pushing off my thighs, and it hurts, so I yelp, but he's too wrapped up in reaction to register what he did.

He flings himself off the bed and seems to be trying to put as much distance between us as possible. His erection is still prominent against his boxers.

"What? How do you know my name?" I ask, finally registering that he said my *real* name. How does he know that? What is going on?

He takes a step back and almost bumps into the dresser behind him, continuing to try to create as much space as possible, but it's no use.

I watch him for a second before he rips his mask off, wasting no time. And that's when I fall back on the bed and cover my breasts in complete shock and horror.

No, no, no. What did we just do?

What. The. Fuck.

"Frankie?!"

Frankie and Rosalia

will return...

LEATHER BOUND

BLACK SILK CLUB

Velvet Rose

Prequel

Leather Bound

Book 1

Untitled

Book 2

Untitled

Book 3

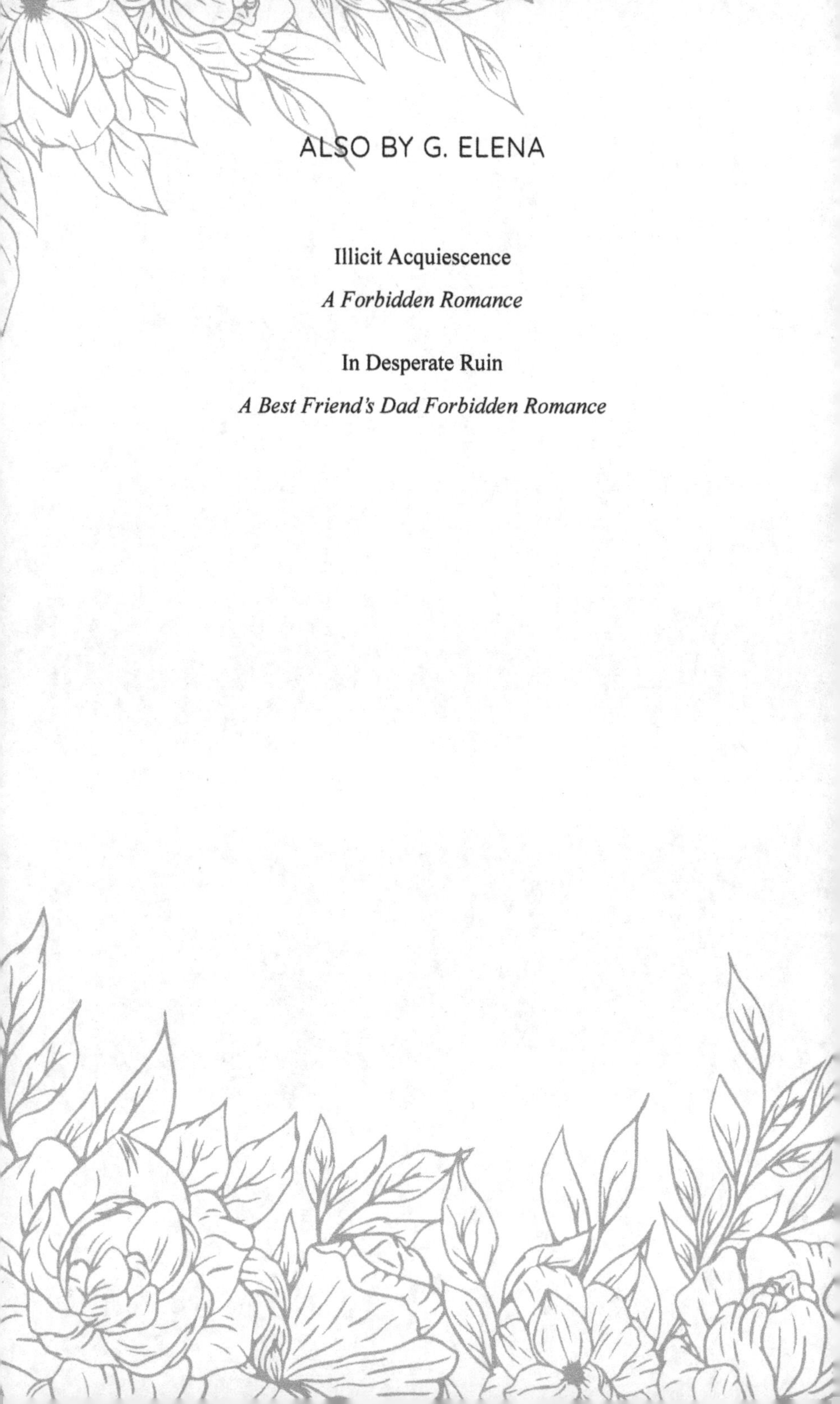

ALSO BY G. ELENA

Illicit Acquiescence

A Forbidden Romance

In Desperate Ruin

A Best Friend's Dad Forbidden Romance

ACKNOWLEDGMENTS

To my readers, I can't say this enough. Thank you for giving this pen name a chance. My forbidden romance novels are something I hold near and dear to my heart and I'm so happy you decided to read them. I wouldn't have come this far, publishing *three* forbidden novels, without you.

To Lizzie, thank you so much for all you do. Not a day goes by where I'm not thankful to have you here with me. You have helped so much in this process and your efforts and hard work are invaluable. Black Silk Club and all that will come from it is because of you and your creative spark—and your willingness to listen to my outrageous ideas. Love you endlessly, love you most.

To Kassidy, thank you for reading the roughest draft ever known to mankind of Velvet Rose and still loving it. Your feedback has helped me become a better writer. I cherish our friendship forevermore.

To my editor Cassidy, thank you again for keeping up with my crazy author schedule and turning my words into magic. My books have become better because of you and I can't wait to continue working with you on future novels.

To Shelby, thank you for the constant support and being there when Black Silk Club was merely a far fetched idea. I appreciate you so much and can't wait for you to read this.

To Emily and Kelsey, thank you for always being so supportive of my crazy antics on both paper and in real life. You guys have truly become my rocks in life and I can't imagine navigating my late twenties without y'all. Thank you for always celebrating my wins, even the small ones. I love you both so much.

To Jenni, thank you for the years of friendship and being one of my first author friends. Thank you for all your help in this publishing world and I hope we can continue to make magic together in the future.

To my hometown friends, thank you for the continuous support states away. From being clueless teenagers to now being full blown adults, thank you for always being by my side. I love you all so much.

To Milo, I hope you're continually proud of me up there. Love you.

To my parents and brothers, thank you for all the support throughout my author journey. I feel so blessed.

ABOUT THE AUTHOR

G. Elena is the forbidden and dark romance pen name for Grace Elena. Please check out her main author page for Romcoms, small town romances, and contemporary romances. She is a Mexican-American author who loves to write with strong Latinx leads.

You can keep up with her on Instagram (graceelenaauthor) or visit her website at graceelenaauthor.com for more insight to her books. If you'd like to get access to sneak peeks to her future novels before anyone else, join her Facebook Private Group "Grace Elena's Vineyard".

KEEP READING FOR IN DESPERATE RUIN

first two chapters

CHAPTER ONE
CLEMENTINE

Tears brim my eyes, cascading slowly down my cheeks. I want to believe that the world *isn't* crashing down on me.

It feels worse. Much worse.

How would anyone feel about their one shot at getting out of this damn town, this damn *country*, being pulled from their reach? It's anxiety-inducing, and I hate that it's become my reality.

"Honey, are you there?" my mom's voice comes through the phone that's still clutched tightly in my hand. I blink a few times before taking a deep breath and bringing it back to my ear.

"Yeah, I'm here."

She sighs on the other end. "I'm sorry."

It's not her fault; it's not really anyone's fault. I want to scream at her, sure, but she doesn't deserve it.

"I can't stay home?" I ask again, knowing the answer.

She's quiet for a moment. "No, honey. I already told your Tía that she can stay there with her family."

My eyes shut tightly, and I find myself latching my free hand onto my bare thigh. My nails *dig* into the skin, leaving marks–soon to draw blood. She's still talking, but I've tuned her out.

The pain distracts me for as long as I can take before I need to clean an open wound.

Feeding into this vice is the only way to stop my thoughts from spiraling. I have nowhere to stay—that's my predicament.

The study abroad program at my university canceled at the last minute with their plans to go to Greece. It was going to be *three* months of sunshine, beautiful landscapes, all the food, and the best time with my best friend, Rosa. That was rare at Frontier University, and I got accepted. I'd be able to finish quite a few credits while there, which was the main appeal for me.

Going to Greece was just the cherry on top.

My mom has been to Greece four times now that she's remarried after Dad died. She loved it so much that she wanted to make another trip out to see me while she and my stepdad traveled Europe this summer. It would be nice to also see him again, I won't lie. I've only seen him on holidays when I travel back home to Maryland. He moved us into this nice lake house once he married my mom when I was fifteen.

College kept me busy to the point where I didn't even have time to go home for the summer. The first summer, I volunteered at an animal shelter, and they gladly paid for summer campus housing. The second summer, I worked at the University for their new student orientation program, and it allowed me to stay on campus for free. Now, this third and final summer before senior year, I don't have *anywhere* to go.

With Tía Selene taking over the lake house with her husband and *four* kids, there would be no room for me. Even if I wanted to go there, I'd be sleeping on the damn floor instead of the room that's reserved for me. I didn't have the fight in me to call my Tía and ask if she could change her plans. Their house flooded in Florida, and since she's my dad's only sibling, she reached out to us. My stepdad, Declan, didn't hesitate at all to open his house to them, which was very kind of him to do.

It didn't make sense for him to say no since they were going to travel all summer in Europe, and I was supposed to be in Greece. So, I *really* couldn't be mad at them. This was just the reality of how much my life sucked.

"Clem!" my mom's voice breaks my thoughts. I pull the phone away, tapping the screen softly to see that we've been on the phone for a solid thirty minutes.

"Sorry, I'm just stressed," I confess.

"Did they refund you yet? You can see if they can use that check for campus housing, *mija*."

I roll my eyes at her attempt to call me her daughter in Spanish. After my dad died, she stopped trying to talk to me in Spanish unless it was to scold me or comfort me in not-so-comforting times. Although I've got her blonde hair, I've got my dad's dark brown eyes and tan skin matched with tons of freckles that I used to get made fun of for growing up.

I love my mom, I really do, but there are times when she does things that make me miss my dad so much. Like talking to me in Spanish. It felt like an *us* thing she was trying to insert herself into. My dad only spoke to me in Spanish. I miss our conversations.

"*Todavía no. No es suficiente dinero, necesitaré más,*" I tell her.

She's silent for a moment, and I crack a smile. She doesn't remember Spanish because she doesn't keep up with it.

"Translate, Clem, this is serious," she scolds.

"*Okay,*" I sigh dramatically. "I said, 'not yet. It's not enough money, and I'll need more'."

"Did it increase from last summer?"

"No, but remember, since it's a study abroad program during the summer term, it's much cheaper than a regular semester. Still expensive, but not as much as it could've been. It wouldn't cover the cost of summer housing."

"Shit, baby, I'm sorry."

"It's fine. I'll figure something out. I'll just find a motel–"

"Absolutely not. I can ask Declan."

"No!" I shuffle to grab the phone. "Please don't. You guys already paid for my study abroad. It's not fair to ask for more. I'll just see if there's a friend around town and ask if I can use the check to pay for some kind of rent if a motel is too expensive."

"What about…" My mom's voice trails off as she tries to remember how many friends I have.

I don't have many. After sophomore year, I secluded myself a lot. I dropped out of the sorority I was in and contemplated changing my major or even *transferring*.

I stuck it out, though, and am really enjoying being a marketing major. It's got fun classes, and I'm set to start an internship in the Fall.

"Rosalía!" My mom's voice finally screams through the phone, and I have to move it slightly away from my ear before I lose my hearing.

"Mom…"

"What? She lives in town, doesn't she?"

"She does." I smooth my hand over my thigh. I take a few deep breaths and think about it.

Frontier University is nestled in the tight-knit town of Sunny Cove, Alabama, near one of the massive lakes. We're close to Birmingham, which is the only big city nearby. We take trips there sometimes for birthday dinners or shopping, but this small town has enough to keep us entertained, especially with it being a University town. Rosa just happens to be a Sunny Cove native, but I haven't been able to reach out to see if she'll stay in town after our trip was canceled.

"Well?" My mom breaks my thoughts once again.

I clear my throat.

"I'll have to see if she's decided to stay after everything that happened. She was going to join me too, remember?"

"Oh, right," she replies.

"I'll figure it out," I reassure her. But my voice cracks, and I know she hears it. Her motherly instinct kicks in.

"Do you want to join us in Europe?"

"No! God no. I don't want to be a third wheel the entire summer. You guys planned this for months, and we all thought I'd be in Greece."

"Yeah, but we also planned to visit you there. We can buy your ticket. It's not a big deal."

"No," I argue.

"Are you sure, Clem?" Her voice is softer now.

"Yes. Please go have your fun with Declan. I'm going to ask for the check today and see what Rosa has planned."

"Alright, baby. Call me if there are any hiccups. We leave in two days."

"I know, I will. Love you."

She says it back and hangs up. I place the phone on the table and glance around the dorm room. I'm supposed to be out already. All of my things, except for a suitcase full of summer clothes, have been shipped back to Maryland. Declan and Mom didn't want to waste any time with me stressing about moving out of the dorm room before my trip. It was a thoughtful gesture, but now I feel like I'm going to have a panic attack without my things.

I get up from the chair and pace the empty room, save for the standard dorm room essentials. The bed is stripped, and my lip quivers. Fuck.

They're expecting my dorm key in the lobby downstairs any second now.

What am I going to do?

My legs shake, and I can't help myself with the dramatics and lean against a wall near the dresser and sink to the floor. I clutch my knees to my chest and press my forehead against them. My heart is already racing, my palms are starting to sweat immensely, and all irrational fears come to the forefront of my mind.

I try to complete the five senses grounding technique I learned in therapy a while ago, but this room is too suffocating to focus. My hands go to my bare thighs again, and this time, they draw blood.

My hands shake as I pat them against my thighs, stomach, chest, and then my cheeks. Why am I nervous? It's just my best friend.

I've got the check in my pocket. What I don't have? Courage. It was fleeting the moment I got news from the admissions office that I could only take *one* of the four courses on campus this summer. The other three were offered solely to the study abroad program. Everything is ruined, and now I'm standing like a beggar in front of my best friend's house.

To make matters worse, I've shown up unannounced.

I couldn't muster the confidence to call or text her about my situation. I felt like a fool and there was no doubt in my head that she'd give me those brown eyes of pity that she does so well for the animals in the shelter.

It wasn't far off from how I felt–a lost puppy. Kicked to the curb with a check in my pocket that might not even be enough for what I was asking for.

I try to shake the nerves before I press the doorbell once. The chime travels through the two-story house, and my feet shuffle in place. I wait a few moments before I start to panic and take a step back. I turn on my heels and walk down the pathway that connects to their driveway. There isn't a car parked, so I know her dad isn't home.

There's the sound of a door creaking open behind me, and I halt in my steps. I turn slightly and see Rosa with her dark brunette hair in rollers. Her brows raise, and I take a deep breath.

"Clementine? I thought you'd be on your way to the airport?" She takes a step toward me, and I close our distance so she doesn't have to walk barefoot on the pavement.

Her brown eyes follow mine, and I try to steady my breathing. "My Tía is staying at the house with her whole family. House flooded or something."

She studies me for a moment before taking another step closer. She slowly grabs my hand that's planted to my side. With gentle hands, she pulls my fingers and rubs them in a reassuring manner.

"That's stressful. Want to come inside? My dad's not home, working on a huge project this week. He'll be here for dinner, though."

I nod my head. "S-sure. You don't mind?"

She smiles. "Of course not, Clem. *Mi casa es tu casa.*" Without another word, she pulls me into her home and I forget how beautiful the Santos house is. The foyer is bright, with tons of light peeking through windows around the door. I haven't been in this house much to remember it since we have the dorms so close, but I've seen enough with random movie nights and while FaceTiming her during holidays. She invited me once for Thanksgiving, but that was when Declan had big plans to surprise my mom and me with a trip elsewhere.

We navigate ourselves to her kitchen, and it's quite a spacious one. It's got a marble island in the middle with four bar stools on one side. She heads to the large fridge to the left and pulls out a pitcher of cold water. She then grabs two glasses from a nearby cabinet. I thank her as she pushes a glass toward me.

"I forgot how nice it is in here," I mumble, looking around to where the kitchen connects with the living room. There's an expensive speaker system there. We tried watching a scary movie last semester on Halloween weekend, but it was so loud and eerie that we had to shut it off. Her dad never seemed to be home whenever I got the chance to come over, so I've yet to meet him.

"Yeah, my dad is proud of his work. He plans to renovate the basement so I can have it to myself once I graduate. That's if I don't run away to LA or New York."

I widen my eyes. "That's so nice of him."

She nods. "He's great. Though he is a little pissed that I'll be home for the summer. Not the fact that I'll be around, but that I'll have to retake those classes somehow. Who knows."

"Rosa…" I start, feeling my heart rate increase with each passing second. "I have to ask you something."

"Sure, *nena*. What's up?" She leans her elbows on the marble island and peers at me with expectant eyes. I shift on the barstool uncomfortably as I rack my brain for the right way to break the news to her.

"I—uh. I need your help. I have this." I pull out the check from the front pocket of my shorts.

The check almost burns in my hands as I drop it on the counter and let her grab it. Her eyes widen as she reads the amount of zeros on it. *Okay,* it's not a lot. But it is to us, at least.

"Woah, I forgot how much it costs to study abroad."

"It's not as much compared to a normal semester, but yes. It's not mine to keep, though."

"So, why are you showing it to me?" she asks, placing the check back down. Without another thought, my left hand moves to go under the counter and latch onto my thigh, fingers already knowing where to go. I know I have to stop and let the earlier marks heal, but today's been too stressful to even bother with the thought.

This is the only coping method that keeps me from doing anything worse. My therapist would be upset if she heard I still self-harm, but what else can I do in such a stressful time?

"I—uh…"

126

"Clementine? What's wrong?" She straightens her posture, and her brows raise. I feel like throwing up. I have to spit out the words before I change my mind and run out.

"It's way too expensive to stay in the dorms this summer and now it's too late to apply to any campus jobs, and I really don't know where to stay. Yes, I have this check, but it wouldn't be enough to get a hotel for three months. There's no room back in the lake house for me, even if I tried to go back. My parents offered to let me join them in Europe, but that's just too much to ask of them. I have nowhere else to go, and you know I wouldn't be asking you or your father if it wasn't urgent." My words come out a mile a minute, and Rosa focuses her eyes on my lips to catch everything.

She's quiet as she takes in my final sentence. "So, what are you asking? Clementine, you know I'll always help you out. You and your family were there for me when I needed it the most."

I think back to when her parents separated right when college started. It was a dark time for Rosa. She was still living at home at the time before she moved on campus that Spring and roomed with me. My mom and Declan offered to take us all to California for spring break, and as much as Rosalía fought not to waste their money on her, they wouldn't take no for an answer.

It was a good way for her to stay away from her home, which was going through ruin. Even though her parents weren't married, they were together her whole life. Her mother moved out in haste, leaving her dad in an empty house. That's when he started renovating the place the summer after freshman year.

He did what he could, in Rosa's words, to have her come back home and be with him. It didn't work, though, as much as he'd like. She decided that living on campus was the best for her relationship with her parents. She barely speaks to her mother now, who whisked herself away to some town in Montana and is now in a relationship with a dude who owns a ranch.

"Can I give your dad this check and possibly stay here for the summer? I'll help with chores, mow the lawn, anything."

Rosalía's lips twitch before she barks out a laugh. "Mow the lawn?"

I nod.

"I'm serious, Rosa!"

"I'll ask him, but don't mention the lawn part. He doesn't like anyone messing with his lawn care, apparently. He got into a heated argument with his neighbor, who has a lawn mowing business."

I can't help but laugh too. "Your dad seems funnier than I remember."

"He's annoying, that's what he is." She rolls her eyes, but her face stays amicable. "Why don't you come for dinner when he's back from work? Wait, where's your stuff? Did it all get shipped back?"

I shake my head. "No, they're letting me keep my one suitcase in the lobby. I almost begged them to let me stay for as long as I could, but they seemed stressed. I overheard one of them saying how there were other study abroad programs that flaked as well."

"I can't believe they let us go through all those meetings and sign up for classes just to pull the rug out from under us!" she wails.

It was stressful for all of us, but it could be even more stressful if tonight doesn't go well. If her dad doesn't let me stay, then what?

"It sucks, but thanks, Rosa. I'll go get my suitcase and meet you back here! Unless you want me back closer to dinner?"

She smiles with a hint of red on her cheeks. "Yeah, I actually have a date with Garrett from the program. Did I forget to tell you I hung out with him a few times after our study-abroad meetings?"

I gasp. "What! You forgot! No wonder you guys kept ogling each other during those meetings."

The blush turns more scarlet on her tan skin. "Don't mention it tonight, okay? Haven't really found a way to tell my *very* protective father about my dating life."

"My lips are sealed." I smile before I get up and place my empty glass in the sink. She gives me a side hug before I head out of her house and call an Uber back to campus. My stomach fills with flutters, but the nervous kind. I'm terrified to know what will happen to me this summer. It'll either be fun and free with my best friend, or I'm going to be a stressed-out mess.

I hope for the best as the Uber arrives and I get in.

CHAPTER TWO

ARLO

My fingers, palms, and wrists are caked in dirt and remnants of oil. Today was one of the more important days of a huge renovation project we have with a client that owns land about half an hour from Sunny Cove. They wanted the house to keep its 'farm' feel while creating a more modern touch inside.

It wasn't too big of a job for me and my men, but it was tough and prolonged work. We were there from six in the morning until almost seven at night. I had to call it quits the moment I realized the time. I promised Rosie I'd grill some steak and make her favorite salsa for dinner, and I can't let her down.

I try to remove the dirt from my hands with wipes I keep in my truck for this exact reason. It takes almost four wipes to get the grime and dirt off to a reasonable state where I can drive without my palms slipping off the wheel. The last thing I need is to crash and miss out on dinner with my daughter. I've spent too long trying to rebuild my relationship with her, I can't chance it.

She'd probably throw the salsa ingredients on top of my grave instead of flowers out of spite. Rosie used to love taco nights growing up, so I try to make it home whenever I promise her it.

It doesn't take me too long to get home and see that some lights are on. I park the truck before grabbing the cooler from the backseat and hopping out. I almost forget the baseball cap on the dash, slipping it on backward.

I slam the truck door before heading to the front door. I used to walk through the garage, but it's become such a hoarding mess after the separation that it's the last place I want to be. One day, I'll have the strength to go in there and clean it out. But not today. I've got steak to make.

The house is quiet in the foyer as I slip off my work boots. I don't miss the suitcase near the coat hanger and I pinch my brows. It might've been Rosie's suitcase she packed before hearing about the cancellation of her study abroad trip to Greece.

I head to the kitchen, hearing some giggles upstairs, and smile. Rosie was torn that her school canceled the trip, but I took it as a sign that it would be the perfect time to bond with her. Ever since the split, it felt like she pushed her mother and me away to cope. I didn't want to force her to communicate if that was her way of healing, so I gave her space. But it's been 3 years, and I want to repair things.

My feet are loud as I make my way down the hall from the kitchen, after cleaning the cooler, to the master bedroom to strip off my dirty clothes. The method is meticulous: there's a hamper right near the door so I can get inside, strip, and not leave any muddy prints or falling pieces of debris on the nice floor. I worked on them relentlessly last summer, so I'd be damned if a muddy print got on it. Beside the hamper, there are flip-flops so I can walk easily to the bathroom without making a mess.

I'm so busy during the week that I rarely want to spend my weekends cleaning this room because of the mess I make, so I stick to this system. I even have a specific body wash for the grime, oil, and mud that might still be on me while I shower.

The house is still quiet as I head to the kitchen after my

shower and whip out the prepared steak: arrachera. It's seasoned with salt, pepper, tons of lime, cilantro, onion, and even some orange slices. The longer you marinate it, the better it tastes, according to *Mamá Santos* recipe. As I chop more onion and cilantro for toppings, I start the salsa as well. There's music drifting from the living room of a playlist I'm not familiar with. It was already playing softly on the TV, so I just turned it up.

I hear footsteps heading into the kitchen, and I turn to see Rosie's small frame as she smiles widely, but her eyes tell me something different.

"*Mija*, I didn't forget about the steak," I rush to tell her as I continue to prep the salsa ingredients and take out a pot to boil the tomatillos in. She watches me for a moment before she clears her throat.

"I have something to talk to you about," she starts. I give her a small smile as I try to stay concentrated on the dinner. It's already nearing nine p.m. and I hate to know that she was probably looking forward to her favorite meal since six. There's a moment of slight worry that I'm focusing on the wrong thing right now, and I silently pray that it's just about the late dinner and nothing too serious. I hear her let out a heavy sigh.

"What's up, baby?" I ask, grabbing what I need for the grill that I forgot to start. Fuck, I need to get the charcoal from the garage.

"Dad, please," she says sternly. I stop in my tracks with the steak on a plate in one hand against my ribs and the other full of grilling tools. Her brown eyes sparkle like her mother's, and I look away briefly before gazing back at her.

"*Mande?*"

She nibbles on her lip for a moment before taking a deep breath. "My friend is here, in my room. She was supposed to go on that study abroad trip to Greece with me..."

"That's nice she's over. She's more than welcome to join us for dinner."

"That's not it…" Her voice fades, and I pinch my brows. She takes another deep breath. "Long story short, she can't go back home to Maryland, and she's kind of stuck here. Can she stay?"

"Like for the night? Of course." I smile.

Rosie huffs out a breath, and I wonder what the hell I'm doing wrong. I look down at the steak and then back at her.

"*No. Escúchame, por favor.*"

"I'm listening," I say with a deeper tone to my voice. I wait for her to gather her thoughts before she spits out whatever is getting her caught up in a web of nerves.

"Clementine, my friend, has a check. Since the program was meant for the entire summer, she wants to know if she can stay with us for a month or two, if not longer, based on her situation. She'll pay for it with the refund they gave her."

Now I'm the one biting my lip in nerves. That's a lot to ask for, but I can see how much this means to my daughter with the way she is looking at me with puppy dog eyes and nibbling on her own lip.

Rosie and I are slowly getting to a good start in our relationship, and I don't want to fuck anything up. Having her friend stay with us for a summer won't be *too* bad. I'm busy as hell during the week, and girls their age go out on weekends, so I'd have the place to myself…

"Ask me again once I've made the steak," I tell her with a warm smile. I don't want to make promises so quickly, plus my mind is on the dinner.

For a moment, I think she's annoyed by my response and will turn on her heels in anger, but instead, she smiles warmly before nodding. "Thanks, *papá.*"

She hasn't called me that since she was little, and my heart almost lurches out of my chest. "Of course, *mija.*"

Before she can say anything else, I retreat to the back of the house to the glass sliding doors until I'm in the backyard. It's vast, with a pool, hot tub, shed for tools, and a makeshift patio.

The grill sits atop the patio, and I place the tools and plate down on the table before assessing the grill to make sure it's clean. I try to clean it after every use so it stays pristine.

I enjoy keeping my expensive things looking nice.

Once I've got that situated, I drag my feet around the backyard, through the wooden gate, and find the extra garage key under a nearby potted plant. I open the garage door and flip on a switch. The walls are lined with boxes, and the center has even more piled in, plus some bikes, a treadmill I don't use anymore, and a small grilling section. I head there quickly, making sure not to look around for anything that might trigger me into a full-blown panic attack. I can already feel the air suffocate me, entering my lungs and wrapping around them, squeezing tightly. A cough slips out of me as I grab the bag of charcoal and I speed walk out of the garage. I slam the side door harshly and throw the key under the mat with force. I look up at the fading orange and pink sunset sky as I take a few deep breaths.

"You can do this, Arlo," I mumble to myself before I head to the grill.

"Rosalía!" I yell from the kitchen, rinsing my hands one last time. I've got the food all grilled and laid out on the island. I don't hear her loud steps down the stairs, so I call her again.

I wait patiently before giving up and leaving the kitchen to head upstairs. There isn't any other reason for me to be upstairs. There's Rosie's room, a guest room, and then a study that Rosie doesn't really use. There's a bathroom in the hallway as well.

Once I'm upstairs, I head to her closed door. I knock on it a few times before I wait. The door finally opens, but it's not Rosalía. It's a very short blonde. Her freckles against her tan skin are like stars in the sky. I try to keep my eyes off her frame as she assesses me.

Her brown eyes widen for a second before going back to normal. I study her for a moment before clearing my throat.

"She's in the bathroom taking off her makeup," the blonde says softly. She shifts in her place, and I look behind her to see Rosie's bathroom door shut. I nod curtly at the girl before turning on my heel. Before I make it to the staircase, I turn my head back and see her watching me still.

"Dinner's ready. It won't be out for long. Got an early wake-up call," I say briefly before heading downstairs.

Within ten minutes, I hear their footsteps down the stairs, as if they're running to the finish line. I'm already eating a taco on a barstool. I moved to the other side of the island to give the girls their space. They reach it, and the blonde is quiet as she takes in the spread of food.

"Wow, this smells amazing!" Rosie smiles before licking her lips and grabbing a plate. She hands one to her friend, who thanks her so softly that I almost miss it. Rosie is too busy filling her plate with tortillas, steak, and salsa to see me watch her friend. Under the bright kitchen light, she's even more breath-taking than what I saw upstairs.

She doesn't have a small frame like Rosie, but she is shorter. Rosie's got maybe five inches of height to her. Her shirt hugs her curves in a delicious way when she leans over for a tong to place some grilled onions on her plate. I shift in my seat from the sight, seeing her lips press together in concentration. She looks up briefly, catching my eyes, and I clear my throat before focusing back on my plate.

Nice going, Arlo.

"We can sit here." Rosie guides her friend to the barstool, and they both plop down.

"Drinks?" I ask, seeing they have nothing yet. Rosie looks up and nods with a smile. Her friend keeps her gaze on her plate. Rosie nudges her, and she looks up.

"Yes, please."

"We've got Sprite, ginger ale, Miller Lite, or Corona," I say as I get up and head to the fridge.

"Miller Lite for me!" Rosie calls behind me. I pull out a can and crack it open for her before I place it on the island, and she reaches for it.

"And you?" I ask, raising a brow at her friend. Her cheeks have a tint of mauve as she catches my gaze, and she shifts in her seat. I watch her for a moment, wondering if she can hear my erratic heart thrumming against my chest.

What the fuck is wrong with me? She's my daughter's friend. I fix my gaze back to the fridge, waiting for her to answer.

"Corona, please," she finally says behind me. I grab a bottle and decide to get two. It's my favorite beer.

I shut the fridge and pull a bottle opener magnet before popping off both caps. She smiles kindly as she grabs it, taking a small sip.

My heart is still thumping loudly as I take a seat. Rosie is making three tacos on her plate, something she's always done. She'd rather have the tacos all ready to eat instead of making one and eating it and then having to prep another one. Her friend, on the other hand, preps one, eats one, and then preps another.

"This salsa is the best," Rosie squeals with delight, and it warms my heart.

"I'm glad you like it. It's *the* recipe," I tell her, taking a bite of another taco I just made. My methods are like her friend's as I finish a taco and start prepping another one.

"You made it?" Her friend's angelical voice pipes up. I stop myself midway from biting into a taco to look at her and nod.

"Yeah, he cooks almost everything he eats. Unless it's for a special occasion and we go to a restaurant," Rosie states from her chair. Her friend whips her head from Rosie to me.

"I've got lots of recipes to try, not enough time," I confess. My mother taught me to cook at a young age, and all the recipes I have are from her. She passed away a few years ago but left me with a dingy binder full of her recipes that I have tucked into a drawer for safekeeping.

"It's delicious," her friend bubbles and takes another bite of her taco. The salsa drips from her lips, and she licks all around her mouth and *fuck*. The sight of her plump pink lips makes my cock go into a frenzy.

I stiffen in my chair and curse myself. *This isn't happening*.

"You okay, dad?" Rosie speaks up, and I finally notice I'm clenching my jaw, and my vacant hand that's not wrapped around the taco is in a fist. I relax my features before locking my eyes with my daughter and nodding.

"Yeah, baby, I am."

"So…" Rosie speaks up as she finishes her tacos. She washes it down with the beer before locking eyes with mine. I raise a brow, and I know she wants to revisit the topic from earlier.

"Mr. Santos," her friend says softly, causing my dick to twitch in my pants. *Jesus Christ, what the fuck?*

I give her a small smile before pressing my lips together. Rosie smiles brightly and looks at her friend with encouraging eyes.

"Clementine León, ask him!" Rosa mocks in a teasing tone. *Clementine León*—the name echoes in my mind, and it's the prettiest fucking name I've ever heard.

Clementine looks at me, a blush creeping up along her neck and then up her cheeks as she shifts in her seat. "I know Rosalía mentioned some of my situation. It would mean the *world* to me if I could pay rent for the guest bedroom. I'll do chores, make sure to even abide by any curfew, and I'll even mow the l—"

"Sure," I say without protest.

Clementine opens and closes her mouth a few times before looking at my daughter, who just shrugs.

"Wow, I expected more pleading," Clementine whispers, looking down at her plate.

"Any friend of my daughter's is welcome to stay. I don't need the money, but if your parents think that is best, then I'll accept it. Make sure they're aware of your decision. I'll give you my number for them to have."

"Thanks, *papá*," Rosalía pipes up, leaning over to squeeze my arm. I give her a smile before looking back at Clementine.

"Of course, sir," she nods quickly.

Sir. The way her mouth pours that word out makes me take a deep breath. I regret my choice immediately in agreeing to let her stay, but I've already told her she can. I can't back out now, and it seems to be the only other option the girl has. It would be cruel of me to kick her to the curb.

"Please, Mr. Santos is fine," I say almost too quickly, and the faintest of a smile hits her lips.

"Okay, *Mr. Santos*."

I finish my beer before tossing the remnants of my plate in the trash, including the beer bottle. I place the dish in the sink, knowing I'll have to do it tomorrow.

Turning to the girls who are already in their own world, giggling about something, I clear my throat, and they both look up. "You guys don't wait up for me. I'm going to head to bed. Clean up after yourselves and leave any leftovers in the fridge."

"Yes, Dad. Goodnight, *te amo*," Rosie says with a two-finger salute to her temple. I walk over and wrap my arms around her from behind. She sinks into my chest, and I kiss the top of her head. She giggles before I release her, and it's awkward for a moment as I stare at Clementine, who twists her head.

"Goodnight, Mr. Santos. Thank you again for letting me stay. It means a lot, and I'll let my mom know before bed."

I nod before tailing it out of there and making it to my bedroom just in time to cover my prominent erection. My head hangs as I take a few deep breaths and think about what the hell I'm doing.

I need to get laid. That's what's wrong. It's been a while; I've been so busy planning this project at work that I haven't had the brain cells to even think about finding someone to hook up with. The dating apps aren't for me, and I'm no longer into the bar scene as much as I was during the beginning of the separation.

After stripping naked, I hop in bed. Sleep doesn't come easy, and I find myself dreaming about pink plump lips and a blonde-haired beauty saddling my waist and sinking herself onto my cock.